THE PURPLES:

Friendships Stitched on a Purple Canvas

AF651747

DEEP JB

BlueRose ONE.com
Stories Matter
NewDelhi • London

BLUEROSE PUBLISHERS
India | U.K.

BlueRose ONE
Stories Matter
NewDelhi • London

For permissions requests or inquiries regarding this publication, please contact:

BLUEROSE PUBLISHERS
www.BlueRoseONE.com
info@bluerosepublishers.com
+91 8882 898 898
+4407342408967

ISBN: 978-93-7310-660-1

Cover design: Daksh
Typesetting: Tanya Raj Upadhyay

First Edition: November 2025

Dedication

"TO THE ABUNDANCE OF THE UNIVERSE" – To each person who found friendships in life and held it to highest regard.

I dedicate this book to all my friends who have been integral parts of my life and spirt of friendships with them would never die.

And,

For every boy and girl who believes in friends and families,

For every spark of hope within friends waiting to take flight–

This book is for you.

This book is also for the **new and future generations**–

Who missed the flavourful days of 'old school' era of 80s and 90s kids, when digital media, social media etc. were beyond a common reach, where a single relationship was valued and cared beyond anything. Through this book I am trying to share a perspective of such old friendships with the new generation, hope it will reach.

And may this book find paths to all readers who believe in friendship, believe in humanity, dare to step forward for loved ones and keep empathy and resilience both at heart that bring the true sense of human being....

Acknowledgement

The idea for this novel was not born overnight. It was seeded two decades ago, during one of my early university days when I was remembering all my friends from college time and to the great level of bonds that we shared in bygone years. While the characters and events were developed with imagination originated from my friends and near ones including myself, the chapters of this book were woven with heartfelt emotions and care that signify not only regards to all my friends but also various life-long learnings, happiness, grief, good & tough times shared together.

When I started initially, the book was left incomplete as my work life evolved and consumed my time more than regular. But in recent years that followed, especially after covid-19 phase when we lost many friends and near ones, I took inspiration from my old days to revamp the stories and started weaving the chapters of the book with an intention to revive the essence of friendship in our lives.

It was only during a more recent months, when fragments of memories began to weave together with reflections and imagination, that this book finally took shape. What you now hold in your hands is a fictional work, but it carries the memories, bonds, emotions, and essence of friendship in our journey, blended with the imagination of many others like us of that era.

Now, as I pen down this note of gratitude, I realize that my list of acknowledgments is long—too long to fully capture in words. However, there are a few heartfelt acknowledgments that are truly essential.

On a professional note, my sincere gratitude goes to **"BlueRose Publishing"** for encouraging me with their support in shaping and publishing this book.

A special and heartfelt acknowledgment goes to **my better half**, for far more reasons than I can count— for her unwavering writing spirit and skills that constantly inspire me, for the spectrum of emotions, life lessons, and shared experiences that have been supporting my perspectives even long before we officially embarked on this journey together.

I can't thank and submit my gratitude enough to all my **friends since my school days, fellow mates, and overseas colleagues**, whose unwavering belief in me and constant encouragement have been a source of motivation. Their words—whether spoken or unspoken—have always carried a silent reassurance, a "**Yes, you can**" energy that has fuelled my journey.

No acknowledgment would be complete without mentioning the **blessings of my parents and all my teachers**. Their wisdom, love, and guidance have shaped every part of my life, and without them, this journey—both as a writer and as an individual—would remain incomplete.

And to you, dear readers—thank you for walking with me through this mini world of friendships. May the chapters remind us that friendship comes in all forms and without them the canvas of life will miss the best colours in it.

Lastly, I must acknowledge the unsung heroes of the modern age—**digital resources and technology**, particularly my **trusty laptop**, which has been my constant companion in this endeavour. Without all these, the words would have remained scattered thoughts, never finding their way onto these pages.

With immense gratitude and appreciation, Deep JB.

About the book:

THE PURPLES: friendships stitched on a purple canvas....

(a fictional novel based on true friendships of eight friends who find a common colour in the canvas of their life journey)

So happy to share this at last – "THE PURPLES: friendships stitched on a purple canvas" finally lives. The first threads of this story were written nearly one and a half decades ago; life pulled me in different directions, chapters sat half-finished, and the voices of Arunav, Ron, Garima, and the rest waited patiently on the page. After my poetry book and a few other books came out successfully earlier this year, I felt the pull to finish what I had begun. Revisiting these old pages, I found not only memories but a promise to myself: to complete this story, which was all about friendship that felt honest, small and eternal. This book is the result of that promise.

"The Purples" are the mixed shade evolved from many colours – eight young people who meet in the city of Guwahati (a city in Assam) and, through music, food, bookfair, late-night conversations and tiny acts of affection and care, form a family. The scenes are modest such as – chai and pakodas, cassette tapes and slambooks, house parties, jamming sessions, friendship bands and even Orkut profiles (the old school era of Facebook) – but the book is built on the large, quiet work of presence: how people keep one another, how they forgive, how they show up, how they protect, how they keep secrets.

Set against the 1980s–90s backdrop before social media smoothed everything into instant signals, their friendships are tactile, steady, loyal and patient. I wanted to capture that texture: the way a song can stitch strangers into friends, how a revealed secret can become a shared duty, and how a farewell can become a lifetime of small rituals.

This book is offered to anyone who remembers or wonders about the taste of friendships that grew slowly, with obligation and joy braided together. It is also for younger readers who may not have lived that era: for you, these pages are a small map of what steadiness looks like, and why a single honest relationship can outlast many loud moments. If the world now prizes speed and spectacle, the Purples insist on something quieter: loyalty, repair, and the courage to remain ordinary together.

Thank you for opening this canvas and walking with them for a while. I hope these friends remind you of someone you once had, someone you still have, or someone you might yet meet. If one line from their evenings stays with you – a shared laugh, a shared meal, a kept secret, a private apology, a friendship band passed on a roof – then this book has done its work.

Table of Contents

Chapter 1: His Last Rain in Guwahati 1

Chapter 2: The Threads of Dreams 7

Chapter 3: When Paths Crossed 13

Chapter 4: The Bookfair Bonds 19

Chapter 5: The Late-Night Visit 25

Chapter 6 – First Union: The Full Canvas 29

Chapter 7: The Rain Before Goodbye 39

Chapter 8: A small Journey with reminiscence 45

Chapter 9: The Gathering at Garima-di's House 55

Chapter 10: The house full of friends and Gifts 61

Chapter 11: Music, Laughter, and Feast 65

Chapter 12: Some Revelations 69

Chapter 13: Restless Currents - Continuing revelation 77

Chapter 14 – The Photograph and the Pause 87

Chapter 15 – Candlelight Confessions 93

Chapter 16 – Midnight Kitchens and Quiet Walks . 101

Chapter 17 – Puri, Prayers, and Practical Hearts 111

Chapter 18 – New Threads in Purple 119

Chapter19 – Sandwiches of Time 125

Chapter 20 – The Orkut – a new digital world ! 133

Chapter 21 – It's time to logoff ! 139

Chapter 1:
His Last Rain in Guwahati

Present Day (in a day in July 2007):

The rain in Guwahati had a way of silencing the streets, of turning the hills into fading silhouettes draped in mist. On most days, **Arunav Kashyap** welcomed that silence–it matched the orderliness he carried within himself. But today, the sound of rain against the tin roof above his small rented room felt heavier, almost as if the city itself was mourning his departure.

Arunav was just at his twenty, tall and lean, with an air of neatness that made people notice him. His bed was always folded by dawn, his books stacked in disciplined lines, his clothes ironed even when no one was watching. He wasn't just disciplined–he was reliable. In every group he had ever been part of, he was the one who remembered the deadlines, showed up on time, never forgets or misses any birthday, and stayed back to help others finish. Friends often teased him for being "too structured," yet they also knew he was the one they leaned on when life tilted.

He wasn't from Guwahati originally. Home was a smaller town further east, but three years ago he had come here for graduation. At first, he stayed in a cramped PG with strangers who rarely spoke to one another but eventually moved into a modest mess where each student had his own small room. It wasn't much, but it was enough.

When the scholarship confirmation letter had arrived a month ago, announcing his admission to one of India's top universities in the capital of India, the news had sparked celebration across his circles. For Arunav, it meant a leap forward, a step into bigger classrooms and larger dreams. For his friends, it meant pride—but also a looming farewell.

For the last four weeks, Arunav's life had been a carousel of farewell meets. His circle wasn't confined to his own department; he was known across the campus, across colleges even, thanks to his volunteering, competitions, cultural fests, and the countless times he had stepped in to help. But there was one group that was more than just "friends." They were family, built not by blood but by the unshakable trust of three years together.

Arunav's seven names, seven souls. Each as different as the seven colours of a rainbow yet woven together into one unbreakable thread of friendship with Arunav.

- **Ananya**, sharp-witted and fearless, the first to debate in class and the first to laugh at herself afterward. Someone who is responsible yet fun loving, one of the prominent threads of their friendships.
- **Meghawali**, gentle and reflective, a quiet poet whose eyes saw what others missed. Somone who displays great energy all the time and a kind heart that melts easily; is a cheerful thread in the stitches of their friendships.
- **Zorika**, bold, tribal roots shaping her strength, teaching them all how resilience could be a way of life. Someone who shares the bright and young energy but with matured actions; is another beautiful thread in their knitted canvas.
- **Ron**, the joker, the heartbeat of every room, whose humour often hid his own storms. Someone with the vibrant energy, undying spirt; is a must needed thread of joyfulness in this friendship journey.
- **Niloy**, calm and steady, the one who spoke less but meant every word. Someone who is full of

knowledge, yet humbled by his actions, is a thread that marks stability in their friendships.

- **Garima (fondly called as Rima-di)**, older and wiser, balancing their chaos with her experience and grounding their impulses with reason. She is the thread that stiches the mark of reliability and guardianship in their friendships.
- **Rini**, the tomboy, with coloured curly hair whose energy and mischief blurred boundaries until one day, much later, her truth would unfold. She is an eloquent thread of their friendships that balances between creativity and boldness.

And then **Arunav** himself, one of the supple threads in their friendships woven into their circle of eight—binding the stitches from every corner and adding his own shade to the shared tapestry, together forming a vibrant canvas of friendship.

For three years, these eight souls had shared something rare. While the world around them wrestled with fleeting flings, breakups, and the endless drama of young adulthood, this group had built something different—a friendship so organic, so deep, that it defied words. They had celebrated festivals together, cried over failures, pulled each other out of mistakes, and cheered louder for one another than for themselves.

And now, the heart of that circle—Arunav—was leaving. Pride filled their hearts, yes. But pride was heavy that day, carrying the weight of a thousand unshed tears.

As Arunav tied the last string on his suitcase, he whispered to himself: "*This isn't the end. This is just the chapter break. We will write more pages together.*"

Somewhere in his chest, though, he knew life would never again be exactly as it had been.

Chapter 2:
The Threads of Dreams

The story of Arunav was never meant to be told in isolation. Destiny had a way of weaving lives together, and by 2007, he had already crossed paths with a group of extraordinary young people. Their bonds, formed between 2004 and 2007, were not forged by convenience or shallow interests, but by humility, shared vision, and the genuine warmth of friendship. Each came from a different corner of the Northeast, from different families, different colleges, even different cultures. Yet, in Guwahati, far from their hometowns, their paths intersected.

There was **Ananya Gogoi**, the aspiring dentist. Already pursuing her DBS, she dreamed of reimagining dental treatments with innovation and compassion. Her sharp focus was matched by a caring heart, always pushing others to look after their health and wellbeing.

Meghawali Bezbaruah (later everyone started calling as Meghali or Megha in short and with love) carried an air of determination. She aimed to rise high in management and leadership, knowing that one day she would channel that experience into starting her own event management company. Organized and ambitious, she had the gift of seeing opportunities where others only saw obstacles.

Zorika Langthasa, warm yet resolute, was walking a new path. She had chosen Social Work, a discipline barely understood in the region at that time. Her vision was clear: to dedicate her life to people, to communities, and to the idea that real change came from empathy and service.

Ron Thomas Hazarika, with his infectious laughter and creative spark, was already known as a self-claimed artist. Beneath the humour, though, lay scars of hardship, including a family setback that had delayed his academic progress. Yet, his genius in drama, theatre, and storytelling made him unforgettable. He was the dreamer who turned pain into art. Currently he was running small creative studio where he coached students for creativity; and was also studying his B.A in 2nd year.

Niloy Baruah was the embodiment of discipline. With aspirations to join the Civil Services, he lived by a routine of study, coaching, and clarity. His punctuality and eloquence came naturally, inspired perhaps by his mother, who had already served in the Assam Civil Services. His path was steady, his purpose unwavering.

Garima Ahmed, known affectionately as *Rima-Di*, was the eldest among them, a practicing lawyer with maturity far beyond the rest. Her dream was bold: to study global law abroad and return to establish a law firm dedicated to social justice and women's rights. Her strained family life with religion interchanged family, had taught her resilience, and her presence in the group often brought balance and counsel.

Rini Wahlang, bold and expressive, dreamed of a future where art and craft could transform lives. She longed to start an NGO that promoted art while championing gender equality and neutrality. Splitting her time between a modern art course and volunteer work with an NGO, she embodied passion in action.

And then, there was **Arunav Kashyap** himself. A boy of many dreams, Arunav had the rare ability to imagine futures beyond the conventional. Though he had missed entry into IITs and AIEEE due to his ambitious selection of course priority, he chose to continue with B.Sc. in Physics, seeing it as a bridge to a new, unconventional world. His vision stretched from futuristic automotive designs to robotics, eco-friendly buildings, and solutions that blended innovation with sustainability. Even in compromise, his ambition was limitless. Alongside, his creative mind never stopped putting down words in his notebooks whenever he finds time. He used to write since school time, used to do art, sketching, painting etc. So, he kept those hobbies alive by participating in many activities in his department and also in other colleges whenever possible.

Though each followed their own academic and professional paths, what tied them together was not just friendship but a shared belief: to give something meaningful back to society. They spoke of innovation, gender neutrality, social security, women's safety, and the promotion of art and culture. It was as though a cosmic thread had connected them all, each born in different places but bound by birthdays that all fell in the same month, as if fate wanted to remind them of their unity. It's December–a month of golden celebration. Along with the festive cheer of Christmas and New Year, when the city glows with lights and decorations, they find an added bonus: countless house parties, laughter, and memories shared together throughout the season. Their birthdays, layered upon the festivities, become reminders not only of joy but of the unity that destiny had scripted for them; as if fate had tied them together with a cosmic thread.

Their journey together was only beginning, but the bonds were already profound. Little did they know that the years ahead would transform them forever.

Chapter 3:
When Paths Crossed

How were all these connections made? Well, some interesting events.

There were few interesting events where these friends found each other. Let's begin with the one well known in the city.

It was around August 2004, in the heart of Guwahati, time for the mid-year Fest at Assam Engineering College. It was more than an event – it was a cultural spectacle, a place where music, art, and youthful energy converged. For Arunav, new to the city and still finding his place, this evening would become a turning point.

At that time, Arunav was staying temporarily with cousins in Chandmari. Friendly and approachable, he had already connected with seniors and peers who opened doors to such events. Through one of his senior cousins, he secured referral passes to the fest's cultural night, renowned for its energy and diversity.

He called **Mon** and **Dhruv** to join him. Mon, a charming local guy from Guwahati, was Arunav's first college friend, known for his gentle nature and easy popularity. Dhruv, on the other hand, was an old acquaintance from his hometown – their bond traced back to afternoons spent at the district library in their hometown. Dhruv was preparing for medical studies in Guwahati, yet his heart longed for moments like these.

Mon, in turn, called his tribal friend **Dimppan** and asked to join this evening. Dimmpan, an ever-ready joyful chap agreed and came with his cousin sister, **Zorika**, and a few of her friends. Dhruv invited his PG mate **Niloy**, who was usually hesitant about gatherings but couldn't resist the allure of the annual fest.

At the college gate, the group united. Their laughter and introductions flowed naturally, as though they had known each other for years. Yet, destiny had more to add to this gathering. As Arunav tried to guide the group through a referral entry, a bold voice stopped him. A girl with curly hair, clad in jeans and a biker's jacket, stood firmly in their way. **Rini Wahlang**, fearless and principled, refused to let them bypass the queue. Arguments rose, voices clashed, until Arunav's senior intervened. With a calm explanation, he validated the passes and, in a gesture of kindness, extended one to Rini as well.

Hesitant but curious, Rini accepted. Inside, the fest was alive with music and colour. Bands from across the world performed, weaving together cultures into a symphony of unity. The group found seats together, their earlier friction slowly giving way to laughter and conversation. Arunav, apologetic and sincere, approached Rini to mend the misunderstanding. She, stern at first, softened at his humility. A handshake later, she was part of the group.

That evening was more than just entertainment. Like the music that blended diverse cultures into harmony, the group itself was beginning to form - individuals from different colleges, backgrounds, and dreams, now sharing a single moment of joy.

That evening's true magnet was the young voice of Assam – "Zubeen Garg", who stepped on stage like a storm that knew how to rule the stage. To Arunav and his friends, Zubeen was not simply a performer; he was the pulse that had first taught them music could be both roar and refuge. Arunav had carried those early Zubeen melodies in his pockets through school corridors, had copied rhythms into the margins of his notebooks, and only later learned to shape words into songs because that voice had shown him the door. For Rini, Zorika and Niloy, in fact for all of them this night was less about formality and more about devotion, like a gathering to celebrate the soundtrack of their youth. As Zubeen hummed the stage with his newly released song of 2004 "Rang...(colour)," the new refrain spilled into the air and the crowd answered like a single living thing: hands rose, feet shuffled, and a thousand little lights blinked in time. The song – about colour and finding & becoming – landed on the group like a summons. Arunav felt it in his ribs: lines of melody that seemed to outline the contours of what he wanted to write, phrases that would later sit on his tongue and refuse to be quiet until he had put them on paper. Around him, faces changed, the strangers became partners in a shared breath; friends grinned with an unguarded recognition, as if the chorus were stitching them into a new pattern like one thread into a new canvas. Rini's eyes shone with a shy, theatrical delight; Zorika's voice, small at first, broke into the chorus, and Niloy who usually watched from the edges, found himself clapping in time, with his laugh loose and bright. The song's colour metaphor did more than sound pretty – it did what music does best: it blurred edges. These different lives, bright and varied on their own, began that night to weave into something larger–a thread of colour made from many threads, each preserving its hue but lending strength to the whole. In that soft, electric dark, with Zubeen's voice folding the crowd like fabric, the friends felt the first drafts of a canvas being painted – not yet complete, but already unmistakably theirs.

The music, the aroma of good food, the rhythm of laughter, and the joy of youthful dreams all blended into an atmosphere that felt larger than life. Passions were reflected in every note, every smile, every shared glance–fuelling an energy that lifted the entire crowd. In that moment, the newly met young souls were not just enjoying an event; they were discovering a bond that felt both fresh and familiar.

For Zorika and Rini, it was a safe harbour of warmth and comfort amidst strangers who no longer felt like strangers. For Arunav, it was the joy of finding a team of friends who radiated an energy so subtle yet so deeply familiar, as if he had known them all along. Niloy and Dimppan felt like companions from another time, suddenly reintroduced through fate, while Dhruv and Mon completed the circle–each presence adding a distinct note to this symphony of new beginnings. Together, they were stitching the first threads of a friendship that promised to grow into something timeless.

As the night ended and the crowd dispersed, **Zorika** extended an invitation to Arunav. Their community had organized a book fair near Khanapara, and she insisted he join the next day, the fair's closing evening. Dimppan supported the idea, offering Arunav a ride home in his old jeep. Surrounded by laughter, chatter, and the company of new friends, Arunav nodded with a smile.

It was the beginning of something far greater than any of them realized: a friendship that would endure, inspire, and transform their lives forever.

Chapter 4:
The Bookfair Bonds

The afternoon sun stretched lazily over Guwahati, and after half a day of sleep recovering from the vibrant college fest, Arunav woke refreshed and excited. The memory of the previous evening was still alive in his mind–the laughter, the music, and those first glimpses of friendship. Tonight, at the Khanapara bookfair, he hoped those connections would deepen. Eager to extend the circle, he decided to call Rini, but his limited outgoing balance stopped him. Instead, he sent her a brief SMS.

It was 2004–a time when mobile phones were still a rarity. Many relied on landlines, PCO booths, or emails checked only at internet cafés. Arunav was fortunate to carry a mobile, as his parents and grandfather insisted on daily calls since he moved to Guwahati. During the fest, numbers had been exchanged. Zorika had offered a friend's number since she didn't own a phone. Rini had one, though she often left it at her PG.

While Arunav was getting ready, his phone was on charging it buzzed. When he checked, it wasn't Rini but from a message from her phone from a friend named Bidisha, replying that She is Bidisha Rini's friend, Rini was unwell, and she couldn't join. Arunav simply replied "Ok, hope she gets well soon" and tucked the phone away, slightly disappointed, but his excitement for the evening carried him forward.

At the bookfair, the buzz of voices, the aroma of street food, and the rows of bookstalls created a festival of knowledge and culture. Zorika spotted him from afar and waved energetically, calling him over to catch a community cultural program in progress. Arunav walked towards her, carrying in his pocket a small gesture—a bunch of handmade friendship bands, a hobby he was known for in college. He thought it a simple but heartfelt way to thank Zorika and her friends for inviting and including him in this cultural gathering. But he could not deliver the token of friendship immediately due to crowd and Zorika was also in hurry in excitement to take Arunav around the corners where their tribal community culture profoundly getting reflected.

As Arunav, Zorika and her friends were moving across the stalls, it was impossible not to notice how Zorika carried her identity with pride. She represented the Dima Hasao community, known for its rich culture, deep traditions, and strong spirit of resilience. The community had long been celebrated for its art, crafts, and storytelling, and the bookfair itself served as a living showcase of that heritage. For Zorika, the event was not just a fair but a symbolic moment of community representation, where literature, culture, and youthful ambition came together on one stage.

As he settled into the event, a familiar voice broke through the crowd: "Arunav... hello, Arunav!" Turning around, he was stunned to see **Ananya Gogoi**, a known face from his hometown. Memories of shared tuition classes during higher secondary days rushed back. They had lost touch when college scattered their circle, but now, amidst the bustle of the bookfair, it felt like a reunion. Ananya, delighted as well, quickly introduced her roommates – **Garima Ahmed** and **Meghawali Bezbaruah**. The introductions soon extended to Zorika and her friends, and the group began strolling through the fair, weaving through stalls, conversations flowing easily as old memories blended with new ones. Ananya fondly discussed with Arunav about her current focus on dentistry and her future plans too. While walking and shuffling through the pages of different books across the stalls they also enjoyed the revived friendships with remembrance of past higher secondary days in their hometown. Under the friendly gesture and ever approachable nature of Arunav, Garima and Meghawali soon became like well-known friends from past rather than new friendships.

Towards the evening's close, a crowd gathered for a street drama carrying a strong social message. The lead performer, with an air of professional flair, suddenly invited Meghawali, Arunav, and another girl from the audience to join the skit. They stepped forward, nerves giving way to the thrill of performing. The play, cantered on education for all and gender equality, ended with applause. The performer thanked them warmly and introduced himself: **"Hi this is Ron"**. With a confident smile, he handed Arunav a small visiting card: "*Creativity Speaks – Ron Thomas Hazarika.*" His modest studio, he explained, was dedicated to teaching creative arts. Arunav was instantly intrigued, sensing a kindred spirit in Ron's artistic energy.

Zorika and her friends later brought over a tray of traditional drinks prepared by women from their community, served with warmth and pride. The evening grew richer with laughter, shared stories, and simple joys. Ananya and Garima clutched bags of books, Meghawali showed off crafts she had bought, and Zorika gifted Arunav a freshly launched community magazine. "Check page 23," she urged. "It has a story written by this girl (she pointed herself with her graceful smile). If you like it, send a feedback letter to our postal address on the back." Arunav promised he would, his smile genuine.

As the night wound down, farewells hovered reluctantly in the air. Monday's classes and routines awaited, but no one wished to let go of the moment. Phone numbers were exchanged, promises made. Arunav reached into his pocket and drew out the handmade friendship bands. He always carries a bunch that was enough to greet all of the new faces. One by one, he offered them: starting with Zorika, thanking her for the invitation, then to her friends, to Ananya, Meghawali, and Garima-di. Finally, he extended one to Ron with a playful note: "I'll count on your creative lessons to make these handmade bands even better. Expect me at your studio soon."

They all laughed, touched by the gesture. While through Zorika, Arunav and his new friends caught their first glimpse of the depth and diversity of the world of Dima Hasao, the bands became tokens of a new circle forming, their silent promise tying them closer together where all their respective cultural background getting submerged into humanly bonds. As they parted, each carried not just books or crafts, but the memory of a beautiful evening and the thrill of friendships just beginning to blossom.

Chapter 5:
The Late-Night Visit

The bookfair evening lingered in Arunav's thoughts long as he was homebound to his room on a city bus. He always travels in city buses and trackers, even though he could easily own a two-wheeler as already offered by his father. Yet, amidst the joy of new connections, one message tugged at his heart—the afternoon replies from Bidisha, Rini's friend, who had mentioned that Rini was unwell. His instincts wouldn't let him rest without checking on her.

He hesitated at first but then sent a short request to his cousin: *"Bhai, could you please recharge my number with Rs. 25 talktime?"* Arunav rarely asked for help unless it was absolutely necessary, but this time felt different. Ideally, no one says no to Arunav as he always helps others. Within minutes, the recharge was done, and Arunav immediately dialled Rini's number. Bidisha picked up again, explaining that Rini had food poisoning, was weak and half-asleep. Curious, she asked, "By the way, who are you? I haven't heard of you before." Arunav smiled as he replied, "We met last night at the fest, and we exchanged numbers." He gently asked if it was possible to visit, mentioning he was nearby. After a quick check with Rini, her friends, and their landlady, Bidisha agreed but reminded him that guests weren't encouraged after 10 p.m. It was 9:15.

Arunav hurried, buying ORS packets and a few packs of Marie Gold biscuits from a medical shop before heading to the address near Zoo Tiniali. After dropping from the city bus and navigating a dimly lit by-lane, he found the house. Bidisha greeted him at the door, and soon he was introduced to her and two other roommates. Rini stirred awake, and seeing Arunav there with small essentials touched her deeply.

While Bidisha prepared the ORS, Arunav filled the room with warmth. He cracked jokes, shared funny observations from the bookfair, and animatedly described the street drama he had joined earlier. The girls laughed, their initial reserve melting away into an atmosphere of comfort and camaraderie. The evening felt like a small gathering of kindred souls.

While they were creating this unknown friendship in this short visit, Arunav also expressed about her meeting with the new members in the book fair. He explained how his old known friend Ananya met her in the bookfair and then a series of friendship grew up that evening.

Before leaving, Arunav reached into his pocket, mentally counting the friendship bands he had still left with. To his delight, there were just enough–plus one extra. With joy, he extended the handmade bands to each of the girls, including Rini. And asked Rini to keep the extra one with her, saying "it's a get-well-soon band" with a giggling smile. The gesture, simple yet heartfelt, overwhelmed her. Here was someone she had only met a day before, already showing care and kindness that felt genuine. In return, she gifted him an audio cassette–half filled with her handpicked Hindi and Assamese songs, the other side left blank for him to record as it was a re-writeable cassette.

At that time, cassettes were treasured possessions. Walkman stereos were in trend, and though CDs and VCDs were available, they weren't accessible to everyone. Rewritable cassettes like this carried not just music, but emotion, memories, and personal touches. For Arunav, a music lover who occasionally wrote songs, the gift was priceless. He also had a nice Walkman which was gifted by his uncle before he left for Guwahati.

The night turned unexpectedly meaningful. On returning to his room, Arunav texted Rini to say he had reached safely. She replied, sharing that another glass of ORS was helping her recover and promising they would meet again soon. With his SMS pack still valid until midnight, Arunav sent messages to the others too—Zorika's friend (a message to Zorika and all her friends), Ron, Meghawali, Ananya, Garima-di—as well as to Mon, Dhruv, Niloy, and Dimppan. Each message carried gratitude and excitement for the friendships forming around him.

Later, lying on his bed, Arunav played the cassette in his Walkman. Familiar melodies blended with the day's memories, painting the night into a beautiful canvas of friendship, music, and hope. It felt like the beginning of something much larger than himself—a journey of bonds, trust, and togetherness that would only grow stronger.

That night, as the cassette played softly in his Walkman, Arunav couldn't help but connect the last two days of newfound friendships with a memory from years ago. He was transported back to his first year of higher secondary, just after matriculation, when he had walked into a new classroom full of strangers—only to discover, by the end of the day, some great bonds that felt instantly organic and lasting. The warmth he felt now echoed that same joy of belonging. Smiling to himself, he whispered, "*I will go and meet them all this time whenever I go back to my town. Not sure who all are where, but tomorrow I will start by sending emails to each one.*" The thought of rekindling old bonds while nurturing new ones filled his heart with both nostalgia and hope.

Chapter 6 –
First Union: The Full Canvas

Arunav liked to collect moments the way other people collected stamps. After the concert, the book fair, and a dozen small conversations stitched across the city, the idea of a proper gathering had been sitting in his mind like a bright pebble he wanted to set on a shelf. The thought of a reunion made him feel as if colours were gathering behind his ribs – seven colours waiting for the eighth to arrive. He pictured those colours as a canvas: each friend a different tone, each laugh a brushstroke. He called them, one by one, and when everyone said yes he felt a small, fierce happiness settle in him. This was not idle company. It was the possibility of patching different lives into a tapestry.

Arunav initially planned a casual meet at Nehru Park area – it was a predictable, comfortable choice: a green expanse ringed by colleges and hostels, easy to reach and forgiving of late arrivals. Nehru Park was where students met between classes, where friendships often began as aimless walks that turned significant. As soon as Arunav mentioned the park while calling around, most of them agreed. Then Garima answered. She paused, and with that practical warmth of hers suggested something different. "Why don't we have it at my place?" she offered. "It's near Silpukhuri. More private, we can sit on the floor, cook, and not worry about passing time." Arunav felt a ripple of surprise and approval – the idea promised intimacy rather than a public scatter. Ananya and Meghali (by now Meghawali turned Meghali for everyone), who were Garima's roommates and shared the house's rhythms, backed the plan instantly. The idea stuck: a home gathering would turn the meet-up into a small retreat, a place where conversation could travel deep without being checked by park closing times. None of them had been to Garima's house before; the prospect of a first visit made the plan feel like an invitation not just to an evening but inside someone else's life.

Garima's suggestion to host at her house near Silpukhuri turned the idea from a map into a route. Nehru Park would have been an easy, public choice, but Garima's house promised a different intimacy – a hall that folded into a kitchen and a bookshelf, a floor that could become a single bed for eight, the quiet safety of a place that felt like a harbour. Arunav liked that. He liked the notion of circular sitting: no one at the head, no one distant. He packed his cassette box the way a priest prepares relics – Zubeen's golden songs at the front, some older recordings he had loved since school tucked behind. If music could be a lantern, he wanted to carry it.

The Sunday they agreed arrived bright and quiet. Arunav was the first to reach, part eager and part curious – this was his first time inside Garima's house, and in that first walk-in he wanted to be both respectful guest and an observant friend. The entrance to Garima's home surprised him with a tidy dignity: potted ferns lined the steps, a small hand-painted sign welcomed guests, and the door opened into a hall rimmed with cushions and low stools. A bookcase ran one wall, its shelves crowded with paperbacks, half-finished journals and a neat row of little objects – a carved flute, a faded postcard, a jar of buttons. The kitchen lay off the hall, its countertops clear, a row of spice jars like medals. Arunav breathed in a contented, private sigh; this was the kind of house he had, in the back of his mind, always hoped would belong to a friend.

Garima appeared in the doorway with a smile that was organized and warm at once. She wore a simple kurta, her hair tied back; and motioned like a host who took delight in small details. "You're early, Nav," she teased, handing him a steaming cup of tea and an impish glance that said she had a plan for everything. Ananya and

Meghali came from the kitchen, wiping hands on their towels, with the practiced movement of roommates who had found choreography in cooking. Plates of chickpeas were already cooling. The scent of mustard oil, mashed potato and small fried fish threaded the air. "We've been at it since morning," Meghali announced, laying out a tray of pithas. Arunav claimed a cushion near the shelf, took in the rhythm of the room and felt the first colour wash across him – organized hospitality.

The music system was an old model but faithful. Arunav set a cassette in, cued the first familiar riff and let the melody bleed into the house. Zubeen's voice carried like the smell of rain: immediate and private, even when the whole street could hear. As the opening notes spilled out, the doorbell chimed and then visitors arrived in a warm comma.

Ron walked in with a pack of juice boxes, a bit careful with his entrance and yet quick to laugh when Garima called his name. Ron's theatrical manners had a softness in the small living room; he hugged Garima like an old friend and then saw Arunav's cassette box and raised a hand in approval. "Curated," he said, as if choosing a line of poetry. Zorika came next, her wavy hair smelling faintly of home; she carried a glass jar of pickles from Dima Hasao, wrapped in a strip of old cloth like a treasure. She offered it with a bright grin and an apology that made the offer sound like a gift and a defiance at once: "Mama says these will make you sing louder." Rini arrived with a paper-wrapped parcel of piping-hot momos, steam hissing out like a small celebration; she carried a ukulele strapped to her back and wore a theatrical half-smile as if she lived on the edge of a joke.

Niloy's entrance was less flamboyant but no less welcome: a stack of magazines under his arm and a tin of cookies he had grabbed from Panbazar. He shook Arunav's hand with the blunt ease he reserved for friends and sat himself down with the assurance of someone who knows the best spot for conversation. Each newcomer brought with them a small story, a small offering; each object became a way for others to read them: pickles that smelled like hills, momos that tasted of steam and spices, cassettes that carried the electricity of a thousand parked afternoons.

The hubbub thickened and then softened as Garima and the two roomies put finishing touches on the food. The floor sprawled like a low banquet table: big plates covered with mashed potato and fried chicken, small fish fry, baskets of pitha, chutneys, yellow dal and bowls of steaming rice. The air hummed with the logic of sharing – hands reached, plates passed, food moved in a slow choreography. Arunav felt the room fold into a communal body; the music was the heartbeat.

There was an ease that only newly born friendships have – the eager, generous trust that assumes acceptance until proved otherwise. Conversations floated and overlapped. Rini, ever the performer, settled cross-legged and plucked a few chords on her ukulele; her small voice threaded the melody of a Zubeen chorus into the room. Zorika's laughter pealed like little bells and she found herself joining in the chorus with a stout enthusiasm. Niloy produced an article he'd flagged in a magazine and read aloud a paragraph that turned into a joke; Ron responded with a small improvised skit about a fictional director named "Babu Bose," and the group dissolved into amused, affectionate groans.

Between bites and laughter, stories began their slow unwrapping. Arunav told the tale of how he had first heard Zubeen, the way a certain song had shifted his idea of rhythm. Garima recounted odd design jobs, Ananya described the long nights of study between rehearsals, Meghali added wry comments and observations. Ron's stories were theatrical and slightly embroidered but always delivered with a warmth that made truth feel safer. Niloy's practical interjections cut through melodrama with well-timed, blunt questions that made them all think.

When it was time for music – because in a house like Garima's, food and music had equal claim – Arunav stood, cleared the small corner where the cassette player hummed and cued another tape. The room stilled in a familiar way: when the first chord strikes, people lean forward as if drawn by a magnet. Rini brought her ukulele to the centre and asked, "Which song?" The cassette answered, and as Zubeen's voice rose the place shifted. It was the kind of sound that made feet tap and palms find a steadier rhythm. Rini's fingers danced on the strings; Zorika sang along, at first tentative, then louder, as if the song had given her permission to fill the air.

Music here was less about performance and more about recognition. It asked nothing of them but to be present; and being present, they became a small orchestra of mismatched instruments and raw voices. Ron beat a rhythm on the rim of a plate; Niloy hummed along under his breath; Ananya, who had been quiet, registered the chorus with a bright, surprised laugh. In that shared sound everyone loosened the last knot of reserve.

Conversation and music braided through the night. The cassette's whir mixed with the soft clatter of plates; sometimes talk paused to let a verse land and then resumed in that fluttering, breathless way people speak when they are newly certain of each other's company. Garima's organized hospitality provided the frame – the cushions, the hot water, the way the kitchen seemed to refill with small miracles – and everyone, in return, brought a little of themselves: Rini's theatricality, Niloy's reason, Ron's drama, Zorika's home-sweetness, Ananya's quiet fire, Meghali's wry wit, Garima's order and Arunav's collecting heart.

By the time the plates had been cleared and the last pitha had been shared, something had been made that no single one of them could have built: a convivial map of friendship, stitched from differing seams. It was less finished than a painting but more alive; it vibrated. On a shelf, someone had left two cassettes side by side – a small, accidental altar – and in the circle the friends sat with the kind of tired satisfaction that follows a day spent making something honest.

When Rini began to hum the final chorus and the ukulele echoed, someone reached for the cassette box and called for an encore. They all laughed and, for a time that felt both long and deliciously short, they were eight threads lying side by side – different textures, bright in their own right, but ready to be woven together. The music, the food, the jokes and the easy silences had painted the first stroke on a wide canvas. It did not yet depict much more than a tone and an intention, but the tone was rich and the intention sincere: they would return to this space, to the music and the shared plates, and build something whole from their colours.

Arunav rushed to his backpack, took out his Digi cam (he often carried his digital camera like a priced possession) and said, "guys let's freeze the frame with a group photo". Zorika excitedly came forward, then others followed. Ron with his artistic touch made a nice frame - all were asked to sit in a line at the edge of the veranda. Arunav set the auto-timer and rushed to complete the line. A nice frame was captured. It became the first reunion - a full canvas where Rini's ukulele and Arunav's Digi-cam remained the witness of this first union getting stitched onto the canvas.

Chapter 7:
The Rain Before Goodbye

The Present day:

The Rain lashed against the tin roof, stubborn and unrelenting. Standing by the window, tea in hand, Arunav watched the blurred outlines of Guwahati streets drenched in silver streaks. He felt a quiet impatience building inside—today was special, the day he would meet all seven of them before leaving the city. Yet the rain refused to let up, as if it wanted him to pause and reflect.

He smiled faintly. Perhaps it was the rain's way of slowing him down so he could savour the memories. And indeed, memories came rushing in—the first laughter at the fest, the strolls at the bookfair, the late-night cassette gift, that first Sunday of first get-together of friends, the countless moments stitched together into a tapestry of three years. With every sip of tea, the moments replayed, bittersweet and vivid.

But since morning, he had kept himself busy—rearranging and carefully packing the gifts he had been preparing for weeks. Each gift was more than a gesture; it was a tribute, a fragment of memory and love he wanted each of them to carry forward.

- **For Zorika**: A handmade notebook with a bold "Z" etched across the cover, decorated with sketches and colours. Inside, dozens of short two-liner poems whispered encouragement and joy. Across the pages were clippings—Zorika's own writings published in magazines and newspapers over the past two years. Arunav had collected them silently, building this surprise. Zorika, the youngest of the group, had blossomed into a writer since that first bookfair in 2004 when her first article got published in the community magazine, and this was his way of saying: "*We value each of your words, and we are proud.*"
- **For Meghali**: A set of three audio cassettes. The first was filled with her favourite mix—MLTR ballads, Zubeen Garg's classics, and few selected songs she had often hummed during their walks. The second was a recording of inspiring speeches from visionary leaders—snippets he had carefully gathered from the internet and taped over late

nights. He believed that these could be mantras for management & leadership which is Meghali's upcoming inspiration and goal. The third cassette was left blank, with a note tucked inside: *"For the voice of your own story. Record it as you grow into the leader you dream to be."*

- **For Ananya:** An apron, hand-painted with soft blue and green strokes and adorned with small dental motifs he had sketched in his playful style. At the bottom, in neat brush lettering, it read: *"For the smiles you will heal, and the dreams you will build."* Symbolic of her future clinic, it was Arunav's way of honouring her ambition to revolutionize dentistry.

- **For Niloy:** A thick, spiral-bound notebook—over 300 pages—that Arunav had painstakingly compiled. Each page carried infographics, notes, and references culled from internet cafés and college IT labs, all aligned to civil service preparation. In a time when information was scattered and hard to access, this was a treasure trove. For Niloy, it was more than a book; it was fuel for his dream of becoming an IAS officer.

- **For Ron:** Arunav wanted something as creative and layered as Ron himself. He prepared a set of bamboo-crafted brushes, delicate and precise, knowing Ron's artistry extended far beyond performance. But the centrepiece was a puzzle—over 100 dismantled pieces, which, when assembled, would reveal a collage of Ron's different performances from the last two years. Each image had been captured on Arunav's small DG-cam, gifted by his father during their trip to Darjeeling back in his first year of higher secondary. That camera, considered an upgraded marvel compared to reel-based Kodaks and Canons of the 1990s, had preserved countless memories. Between the puzzle pieces, Arunav inserted snippets of Ron's monologues, ensuring that every fragment carried both a picture and a word, a reminder of art born from perseverance. It was not just a gift, but a mirror of Ron's journey, pieced together with admiration.

- **For Rini**: Bold, vibrant, and unapologetic—her gift had to reflect her essence. Arunav chose a *gamusa*-printed jacket with the phrase *"Bold & Beautiful ~ Courage at Peak"* emblazoned on the back. It was exactly the kind of attire Rini loved, a statement piece. Alongside it, he added a Walkman purchased from a niche shop in Paltan Bazar. To give it a handmade soul, Arunav replaced the front flip cover with bamboo craft, hand-painted in eight colours like a rainbow—but in a deliberate, different order. At the bottom, a phrase read: *"Gilbert's way."* It was cryptic, meant as an inspirational code only Rini would understand and interpret over time. Arunav hoped it would not only make her smile but also ignite the fearless spirit she carried within.

- **For Garima-di:** Perhaps the hardest to decide. Rima-di was selective, discerning, and already far ahead in her professional journey. Arunav resolved to gift her knowledge—the kind that would feed her dreams. He gathered international case studies of law related to women's rights and social justice, printing and binding them into a handmade book titled *"Collection of Case Studies from the World's Famous Law Professionals."* The cover was carefully hand-designed, carrying his respect and thoughtfulness. At the end of the book, he left one chapter blank, titled: "*Chapter – Story from 2012 by Garima Ah.*" It was Arunav's subtle way of saying, "*Your story is waiting. Fill it with your own landmark case.*"

Each gift was not simply an object, but a piece of himself, shaped with patience and love over weeks. They were tokens of memory, of laughter, of unspoken promises. As the rain continued to pour, Arunav glanced at the carefully packed bundle beside his bed. His heart raced, not from the storm outside, but from the anticipation of giving—of watching his soul friends unwrap not just presents, but the depth of his affection for them.

His day, filled with hope, aspiration, and affection, could not be stopped by the stubborn rain. Just as he wondered how he would manage to get to his friends, Dhruv arrived with Dimppan in the latter's Jeep. This time the vehicle was fitted with a freshly repaired hood, strong enough to shield them from the downpour. Dhruv called out with his usual cheer, "Bro, sorry I vanished this morning. Dimppan and I were busy fixing the hood, and now we'd love to drop you at your destination. I'm sure they're all waiting for you. And then we would head off." Arunav smiled in relief—it was a perfect rescue. During such rains, Guwahati streets often drowned in waterlogging, and finding an auto or taxi was nearly impossible. His destination lay near Shilpukhuri, where flooding was always a risk. Together, they loaded his bundle of gifts, with Dhan—the caretaker of the building—volunteering to carry the bag under a large umbrella. With gratitude, Arunav climbed into the Jeep, his heart steady with joy as they set off through the rainy streets toward his waiting friends.

Chapter 8:
A small Journey with reminiscence

The Jeep moved steadily through the rain-slicked streets of Guwahati, carrying Arunav toward Garima-di's house, where his friends were already waiting. His eyes lingered on the blurred city lights through the drizzle, but his mind wandered elsewhere–to the countless journeys he had made across this city in the last three years.

As they drove over the Guwahati Club Bridge, his thoughts deepened. He had crossed this bridge more than a thousand times, often pausing at its centre to gaze at the tangled railway tracks below. The clamour of trains, the restless crowd, the endless motion–they had always fascinated him. Today, those tracks felt like metaphors for life itself: confusing, noisy, sometimes delayed and difficult. Yet, just as the trains always found their way forward, he remembered how each of his friends had faced struggles—setbacks, financial strains, family hardships, health issues—and together, through empathy and unity, they had managed to overcome them all.

As the Jeep rolled past the Guwahati Club crossing, Arunav's gaze caught familiar corners of memory: the small bakery where he and friends had shared countless cups of chai and samosas, the Archies Gallery they often wandered into out of curiosity. They could rarely afford its products, but even a visit sparked creativity and wonder, filling them with inspiration.

Arunav leaned back in the Jeep's seat and, as rain-smoothed lights blurred past the window, he turned to Dhruv with the kind of sudden nostalgia that made voices soften. "Do you remember the studio in that lane?" he asked, nodding toward the narrow alley after some shops they passed by the Archies Gallery, and the question opened a small door in all of them. Dhruv's grin broadened as memory matched his cue. "Which one – the little one with the hand-painted sign and the poster of some band nobody knew?" Dimppan laughed from the front, kicking an imaginary pedal, and Arunav smiled at the picture of it: a cramped room that smelled of varnish and cigarette smoke, a recording mic that looked like a relic, and a desk stacked with cassette cover mock-ups that felt like treasures to a young man who kept songs in envelopes.

"Yes," Arunav continued, "that very lane. I remember it like it was another life – it was 2004, I had just come to scout for a PG and I found that studio by accident. I walked in with nothing but questions and a head full of half-finished songs." He spoke as if unrolling a small map. "I wanted to know how a studio worked, whether my songs could live beyond the pages of my notebooks. Inside, there was this designing desk where they made cassette covers – bright paper, hand-drawn art, mock-ups pinned like flags. The posters of newly released albums of his favourite Zubeen Garg made me so intrigued that I could not resist but to touched them with joy. I must have stood there, staring, because the assistant-dada – a gentle man with ink-stained fingers – saw me and was kind enough to invite me in. And that same time I remember your call, Dhruv – you said you were coming to Guwahati next week; it was like a call just on the bull's eye. And I told you immediately to bring the old copies of my songs and poems from my parents, from my house." He then continued "You showed up with those notebooks, and, for some reason, my favourite comic books too."

Dhruv barked a laugh and lifted his hands as if displaying the old treasures: "I still remember lugging in your poems and a bag of comics full of your favourite superheroes– Doga, Super Commando Dhruva, Bhokal, Nagraj.... even those Twinkle issues of Supandi And Sikari Sambhu you loved as a kid."

Arunav's eyes softened at the memory. "yes bro, you brought them all," he said, "and immediately the next day we sat on the studio floor like conspirators, reading lines aloud and arguing about whether a good chorus could save a bad verse. The assistant-dada kindly explained the process: how the tape was recorded, mixed, spliced, and then transferred to a cassette; how cover art had to shout in twenty seconds to sell a music idea to a passerby; how even silence in a recording was as important as the notes. He said we could do our own songs if we came prepared, but at that time I felt entirely amateur – too raw. I remember myself saying, 'No, da, not yet. Only good writing won't work; I have to learn how to shape a sound and present it properly. I'll come back when I'm ready.'"

The Jeep hummed along and the men fell into a lull before Dhruv chimed in with a detail that made everyone laugh out loud: "And then you did come back – with a stack of poems and a chorus someone later stole as their demo." Dimppan elbowed him and the laugh softened into the private kind that stitched friends together. Arunav's voice turned reflective again. "After the studio, we spent afternoons at the library – that old municipal library where the ladies in the counter tolerated our noise because we came to read and not just to loiter. It was where I re-discovered you properly, Dhruv; you remember we spoke about an old library incident at our hometown? Dhruv uttered "which one....the comic girl?"

Arunav recalled as he started "you arrived late one rainy day with a comic in your hand and that quiet, easy manner of yours. I remember we swapped collections like offerings: your comics for my Twinkles and vice versa; and your borrowed Twinkles for my battered Penguin paperbacks." Dhruv's expression went a touch distant, and then warm. And Arunav looking at Dimppan started the story of Dhruv "There was a girl who came to the library sometimes – always reading the same section, quiet, poised. Dhruv used to notice her, and me too of course," he said, the admission sounding young even now. Arunav smiled, remembering a scene like a careful snapshot. "You liked her badly enough to call me in a panic," he teased Dhruv. "She used to come on Tuesdays. You wanted an excuse to talk to her, so I loaned you a comic – one of those dramatic Dhruva issues – and told you to 'accidentally' drop it near her and then I will shout "Dhruv, you dropped Dhruv" to catch her attention. And we did the same, and then you spoke, and her smile was the rest of the story."

Dimppan, never missing a chance to needle, raised his voice just enough for the passing pedestrians to hear. "So Dhruv, was she your girlfriend then... and still?" he drawled, earning a chorus of mock outrage from the others. Dhruv reddened, half-pleased and half-exposed, but before he could answer Arunav, with comic precision, cut in with a cliffhanger: "She tied Rakhi on you later. Ha ha ha.."

The words landed like a joke with the light sting of truth; everyone burst into laughter. "She tied Rakhi?" Dimppan repeated, eyebrows shooting up. "That's the headache of a lifetime, man." Dhruv scoffed, pretending to be wounded, "Yes, she tied Rakhi – either family tradition or the most gifted of pranks." The laughter settled into a warm silence; memories had a way of turning the small edges of embarrassment into soft gold. Arunav added in a quieter tone, "Those days taught us how to make beginnings with awkward hands. The comic trick wasn't about cunning; it was about creating a bridge – a small permission to speak. And later, when we went back to the studio with more songs, more courage, the assistant-dada clapped us on the back and said, 'Now you are ready.' Not because we were perfect, but because we returned with patience." He paused and watched the streetlights smear into streaks of water reflection due to the wet roads. The rhythm of that memory had a cadence – rent, poems, comics, an awkward conversation that became a friendship, a studio that taught them the discipline of craft.

Dimppan, always ready to return the thread to the present, nudged Arunav and said, "And do you remember those Saturday at the physics lab roof when you used to be at department for extra works, and I joined sometime to participate into the badminton challenges on the backyard of the department?"; Arunav nodded. Dimppan continued "and then those late practices on the roof with your songs, we thought we were secret composers, but the custodian heard us and joined in."

The Jeep filled with a fresh burst of laughter at the recollection of clumsy chords and improvised lyrics. Arunav's smile softened into something like gratitude; the old days were a patchwork of small generosity and daring. He felt the warmth of the memory wrap around him like a shawl as the clouds in the sky slid by. And in that warmth, he heard, almost before it arrived, the buzz of his phone—an interruption that would fold the present back over the past.

His phone buzzed, pulling him back from memory. It was Rima-di. "Oi kot asa Arunav, mur chicken ready, baki buro palehi, ami roi asu" (Hey, where are you Arunav? My chicken is ready, the others are here already, and we're waiting for you). Arunav smiled, replying, "Ahi asu ba, maybe 10–15 minutes more to reach." She cautioned warmly, "Alap pani hoise, tumi carefully ahiba while stepping near the pavement" (Some waterlogging is there, be careful while crossing the pavement).

Her words triggered another memory from 2005, a rainy day much like this one, when Ananya had slipped near a waterlogged pavement and badly injured her leg. The group had rallied around her, hosting jamming sessions and cooking meals at home while she healed. They had turned hardship into celebration, proving the strength of their bond.

The Jeep slowed as they reached Nabagrah Road. Dhruv and Dimppan dropped Arunav near the bylane leading to Garima-di's house. The rain had finally stopped, the skies beginning to clear. Dhruv grinned, "Dude, have a good evening. We're off to the Shillong event now, the one I told you about with Dimppan's friends. But we'll meet tomorrow afternoon as promised." Arunav reminded them, "For sure guys, but remember, my flight is early morning the next day—I'll leave at midnight tomorrow. I've already told Mon and his club friends to join us, it'll be our last big gathering before I go."

They exchanged a hi-five, laughter bubbling through the fading rain. "Safe travel guys, drop a message when you reach," Arunav said, before hefting the heavy bag of gifts and heading down the by-lane.

As he walked, his heart swelled with a quiet realization. Over the past two to three years, their relationships had matured beyond mere companionship. They had become a family, bound not by blood but by trust, support, and shared humanity. Differences of gender, culture, and ambition had never divided them; instead, they found strength in diversity.

In an era where competition was growing and digital distractions rising, love-affairs were in lime-lights with stressed relationships, theirs was a rare kind of friendship—pure, organic, and unwavering. For Arunav, it was more than just bonds of youth; it was a lifelong foundation built on love, care, and the courage to walk together through every storm.

Chapter 9:
The Gathering at Garima-di's House

The atmosphere inside Garima-di's house was already alive with warmth and anticipation. Though the rain dampen the outside, the walls of the home vibrated with laughter, creativity, and the quiet excitement of friends waiting for one of their own.

At the entrance lobby, a surprise awaited: a caricature face of Arunav with the bold caption "*Bhai Ja Raha Hai...*" sketched in Ron's unmistakable style. His knack for humour and art gave the gesture a touch of mischief and affection, ensuring that Arunav would be welcomed with smiles. Just beyond, near the hallway leading into the main hall, a water pot brimmed with purple-lavender flowers. Resting beside it was a small paper note that simply read: "*we are 'The Purples'.....*"

This name "The Purples" had first been suggested by Arunav for their group during one of their last house parties few months ago, an idea tossed out with both thoughtfulness and vision. Everyone had loved it, but life had quickly swept them into exams, work, and responsibilities, leaving the name without an official claim—until now. Purple, as a colour, held depth and history. It symbolized wisdom, creativity, ambition, and even a sense of magic. From ancient Tyre, where rare dye was extracted from sea snails and exalted as a mark of royalty, to its place in Homer's *Iliad* and Virgil's *Aeneid*, the shade had always been a sign of something beyond ordinary. For Arunav, purple carried another meaning too—it reflected inclusivity and identity. On the pride flag of LGBT community, purple symbolized non-binary gender identities; in the bisexual flag, it was the blending of red and blue. His choice of the name "*The Purples*" was not casual—it was a symbol of creativity, equality, and the thoughtful spirit that defined their group. Now, with the flowers and note, it became official.

As the entrance opened into the main hall, the scene inside was just as magical. The large room had no sofas or chairs in use that evening; instead, everyone would sit together in a wide circle on the floor, just as they used to in the early days. This was their sacred arrangement, one that had held countless evenings of book readings, storytelling, Ron's impromptu skits, or jamming sessions when Rini strummed her ukulele and Niloy played his mouth organ. The circle was symbolic—it reminded them of 2004, when on a Sunday evening, they all (all eight friends) had first formed the foundations of their bond in this house.

At the centre lay a plate full of homemade cookies, lovingly baked by Zorika, and a jug of refreshing *nimbu pani* prepared by Meghali. Both were small gestures, yet they carried the essence of comfort and care that had always defined the group. Last year, Zorika shifted to Garima's house when her other mates left the city and gone back to Dima Hasao. Zorika being the youngest and so organized, easily found welcoming place in Garima's house where with Ananya and Meghali it was place of tranquillity.

While waiting for Arunav, one by one, the friends began recalling their memories with Arunav. Zorika spoke softly of how he had once cut and saved her published articles, always encouraging her to keep writing, helped her many a times by accompanying in many college events as a guardian in night returns. Meghali remembered the long walks and the endless debates they'd shared, where he always left her with fresh perspectives. She fondly remembered how he arranged music systems, customized cassettes with dubbed voices many a times to help her in many events.

Niloy recalled the time Arunav had rushed to help him when his scooter broke down on a rainy evening, walking miles together just to make sure Niloy got his PG safe. He also mentioned Arunav's persistence in gathering information for his friends and seniors from Delhi & Mumbai, that had been a help in IAS preparation, calling him both a helper and motivator.

Ananya shared her memory of their library days, when Arunav would always manage to track down the rarest reference books and then willingly lend them out before using them himself. Also, often he teased her with a visual of smelly mouths and bad teeth which she would need to play with always. She also remembered, even they travelled back to hometown together in night buses many times, like a protector to her. Always caring and fun to be with.

Rini spoke about the many evenings they spent singing and sketching together, how Arunav would hum along to her ukulele even if he was off-tune, and how those moments made the group feel alive. Even she recalled that many of her stage performances were with lyrics from Arunav, but he never asked for any due credit. And she hummed saying "many more secrets that he nicely kept so far", with a smile. Then she fondly recounted his late-night visit with ORS and biscuits, which was the start of this friendship.

Garima-di, smiling warmly, remembered his quiet respect for her counsel, how he never hesitated to discuss serious issues and yet always left the space with a joke or a thoughtful question. Also, she remembered those Sundays when he used to get some fresh small fishes and asked her to prepare "patot dia mas" (a small fish dish steamed with spices wrapped in banana leaf); which she never hesitated to do so.

Together, these stories painted the same picture—Arunav as someone who was always present, always willing to go the extra step, whether in small gestures or larger acts of care. Each memory, though different in detail, echoed his selflessness and the quiet strength he carried into their lives.

Ron, of course, kept breaking the emotional rhythm with his jokes, imitating Arunav's serious expressions or poking fun at their "too sentimental" circle. His humour filled the room with laughter, balancing the nostalgia with joy. Together, their voices blended into a tapestry of love, gratitude, and remembrance.

Then, just as the conversation reached its peak, the calling bell rang. The group fell silent for a moment, glances exchanged. The moment had arrived. At the doorstep stood Arunav, with ceased rain-drops still glistening on his shoulders, a bag of carefully wrapped gifts in his hand, and a smile that carried the weight of three unforgettable years.

Chapter 10:
The house full of friends and Gifts

The rain had slowed to a drizzle by the time Arunav reached the doorstep. He paused for a moment, the heavy bag of gifts resting against his leg, before carefully slipping off his wet shoes. His eyes lingered on the caricature pinned up in the lobby–Ron's playful sketch of his face with the caption *"Bhai Ja Raha Hai..."* He chuckled softly, shaking his head, admiring how Ron's humour could capture the heart of a moment with so little.

"Guys, I am here. Where's a towel?" Arunav asked, half in jest but fully mindful of his tidiness. He had always been the one to fuss over order, to make sure no space was left messy because of him. Before anyone else could respond, Zorika rushed forward with a towel, her eyes gleaming with excitement. Arunav couldn't resist teasing her; he shook his head, sprinkling droplets of water onto her. Zorika squealed and laughed, hugging him in mock protest, the warmth of the moment eclipsing the chill of the rain.

As he stepped further into the lobby, his gaze fell on the lavender-purple flowers floating gracefully in the water pot. He bent slightly, inhaling their delicate fragrance. His smile widened—colour, scent, vibrancy, these things always spoke to him, always made him feel that a place carried life. Then his eyes caught the small paper note beside the flowers: "*The Purples.*" He froze for a second, his chest tightening with quiet joy. The name, once just a suggestion, now stood affirmed in front of him, embraced by all. He touched the note gently, his mind filling with the layered meanings—the wisdom, creativity, equality, and hope the colour purple represented. It was no longer just a name; it was a declaration of who they were together.

He walked into the main hall where his friends sat in a wide circle, their laughter and chatter filling the room with familiarity. Without any speech or fuss, Arunav carried the bag into the centre, knelt down, and began handing out the carefully wrapped gifts. He didn't explain, didn't narrate the stories behind the gifts; he simply passed them one by one with a warm smile, his eyes holding more meaning than words could.

For a moment after, silence filled the room. Each of them sat still, holding their packages, their gazes soft and distant as they slowly unwrapped the gifts. The rustling of paper seemed louder than usual. As the surprises revealed themselves, emotions welled up. No one spoke immediately; instead, the air itself seemed heavy with gratitude. They looked at Arunav, then at one another, their expressions saying what words could not.

Finally, voices broke the silence–first soft, then flowing. They began to thank him, not just for the gifts but for the thought, the care, the patience stitched into every detail. Each one expressed what the gesture meant to them, their interpretations as unique as their dreams. Some spoke through laughter, others with trembling voices, but all of them knew these were not just presents. They were pieces of Arunav's heart, tokens of memory and faith to carry with them as they moved forward in life.

The room remained hushed yet full–of love, of gratitude, of bonds that could not be spoken into simple sentences. In that circle, on that rainy evening, they all knew their friendship had reached a depth beyond seasons, beyond years.

It was more than an exchange of gifts; it was the moment when their companionship crystallized into something enduring. The silences, the smiles, the tears, and the laughter all carried a shared understanding: that they had built a family out of friendship, one that would stand strong no matter how far their paths diverged in the future.

Chapter 11:
Music, Laughter, and Feast

To break the emotional air into happy atoms, Ron leapt into action. With perfect timing, he launched into one of his favourite antics–mimicry. He addressed the circle of friends in the gravelly voice of Nana Patekar, complete with stern expressions and sharp gestures. Just as everyone burst into laughter, he shifted into the soft-spoken tones of Amol Palekar, and then without pause, transformed into the ever-expressive Johnny Lever, poking fun at the girls in his exaggerated comedic style. The room erupted in laughter, the earlier silence dissolving into waves of joy.

Rini, feeding off the energy, picked up her guitar and strummed the opening chords of her favourite Enrique Iglesias song. She was quite good with strings, be it Ukulele or Guitar. The notes filled the air with rhythm and warmth. Niloy quickly joined in with his mouth organ, adding a soulful undertone, and within seconds Meghali and Ananya chimed in with their voices. From the kitchen, Rima-di hummed along while warming dishes, her voice blending seamlessly with the impromptu performance. Finally, Zorika lifted the harmony with her sweet, melodious tone. Arunav, unable to resist, added the percussion—tapping his hands on the table and his legs, creating a beat. Then the western musical aura merged into Assamese soulful melodies. What began as a spontaneous act of mimicry had transformed into a full symphony of voices, strings, and rhythm. Their circle was no longer just friends sitting together—it was a band of souls in perfect sync.

As the music softened, conversations and jokes filled the space again, flowing like the rain outside that was catch & dog, had now reduced to a drizzle. Soon, Rima-di brought out the first dish, and the aroma spread through the hall: Assamese-style chicken cooked with bamboo shoot, her signature recipe, steaming and irresistible. Beside it came a platter of golden fish fry, followed by crispy *bengan fry* that carried the taste of home. Zorika presented a neatly crafted salad, vibrant with colours and freshness, while Meghali added her specialty—yellow dal cooked with *o'tenga* (elephant apple), tangy and comforting. Ananya brought out a bowl of fried potatoes tossed with neem leaves and green chilies, a rustic yet soulful dish and Arunav's favourite munchies. Niloy proudly pulled out bottles of Coca Cola and Fanta from the fridge, which he had stocked earlier. Not to be left behind, Ron went into the kitchen and emerged with bowls of homemade pickles—gifts sent from his home the week before, he kept them here at Rima-di's house—each bowl releasing its own sharp, spicy aroma.

The dishes were placed at the centre of the circle, and everyone gathered around, serving one another with laughter, teasing, and affectionate banter. Each dish told a story—not just of flavours but of the people who made them, their backgrounds, and the way they shared their culture through food. In every bite, there was comfort, tradition, and friendship.

While the laughter and chatter carried on, Arunav's phone buzzed several times. Messages poured in from his college groups, friends from other colleges, and even old acquaintances from social circles he had touched. Each message carried warmth—farewell wishes, nostalgic reminders, invitations to meet again. He glanced at them in between conversations, smiling quietly at the realization of how many bonds he had created and nurtured in Guwahati.

The night deepened, but the energy in the room stayed high. After plates were cleaned and stomachs filled, the group wasn't ready to stop. Rima-di, always the spirited one, suddenly pointed at Ron and challenged him: "Come, let's see how good you are at carrom!" The room erupted in cheers at the idea. Quickly, a carrom board was placed on the floor. Arunav eagerly joined Rima-di's side, while Ananya jumped to Ron's support, balancing the match teams perfectly. The rest of the group gathered around, forming a noisy audience, their laughter echoing as the first striker hit the board. Meghali played the FM channel as this was the time for her favourite show at FM full of good Assamese music and engaging talks by the RJ.

The room buzzed with excitement, teasing, and playful rivalry as the match began. In that circle, with food still fragrant in the air, music lingering in their ears, and laughter flowing freely, it felt like time had paused. The night belonged to them—an evening of joy and togetherness before the dawn of new journeys.

It seems an evening chapter closes with their fingers poised on the carrom coins, the striker sliding, and the air thick with playful competition—a perfect bridge to the next unfolding of their story.

Chapter 12:
Some Revelations

Time had flown that evening, and as the rain softened into a rhythmic backdrop, it was time for late evening chai. Niloy volunteered to fry some onion pakodas in the kitchen, and Zorika, always happiest when cooking and serving, eagerly joined him. Meanwhile, Ron appeared distracted–his phone buzzing more than usual, his face carrying hints of urgency even as he tried to stay in the mood of the evening. Meghali raised her voice, "Guys, who wants milk tea and who wants black *adrak* tea?" Most hands went up for milk tea. Ananya and Rima-di, sitting close to Arunav, busied themselves asking about his family, his college team, his upcoming move to the new city, and teasing him: "So, have you found someone special yet, or will you keep matchmaking for others while staying out of the so-called relationship mess yourself?" Arunav laughed it off, dodging their playful questions.

Amid all these parallel scenes, Rini sat quietly in one corner. Her eyes rested on the bamboo-covered Walkman Arunav had just gifted her, its surface painted with eight vibrant colours and inscribed with the code *"Gilbert's way."* The sight of it pulled something deep inside her—an emotion she had long suppressed. She wanted to speak, but hesitation gripped her. Her gaze tried to catch Arunav's, hoping he would understand the unspoken words. Arunav, distracted by conversation, looked at her only occasionally, unaware of her silent plea. Finally, their eyes locked. Rini blinked twice, slowly, with intention. Arunav understood. The gesture carried weight—it was as if she was saying: *"Let's tell them. It's time."*

He hesitated at first, cautious of breaking the flow of the evening. But as he glanced back at Rini's determined eyes and then at the eight-coloured Walkman, he decided to act. Rising from his spot, he called out, "Guys, sorry to interrupt. But I think this evening is about to become even more than what we thought. I feel a revelation coming in..."

The room fell silent. Everyone looked at him in confusion—everyone except Rini, Ron, and Rima-di, whose expressions subtly shifted, as though they had anticipated this moment. From the kitchen, Meghali shouted, "Yes, yes, go on, Nav... what's there?" Zorika added eagerly, "I'm equally curious!"

Arunav walked straight to Rini, knelt down, and hugged her tightly. At once, the strong, independent girl they all admired broke down, tears streaming freely. The room froze in stunned silence, the only sounds being the faint music from the FM radio and the boiling of tea water in the kitchen. Gently, Rini wiped her tears and whispered, "Yes, there is something you all don't know about me. Arunav has known... but the rest of you don't."

Ananya leaned forward, worry etched on her face. "Hey, are you alright? I've never seen you this emotional." Ron, momentarily pausing his phone activity, urged softly, "Rini... share it with us."

Rini raised the Walkman in her hand, pointing specifically to the colourful palette and the inscription. "This," she said, her voice trembling yet filled with conviction, "this is my truth. Do you know what it means?" She looked around the circle, searching their eyes. Niloy entered from the kitchen, curious, and said without hesitation and with his knowledge, "LGBTQ? We know you... you support LGBTQ, right? What's new there?" Zorika frowned, clearly unfamiliar. "What's LGBTQ?" she asked. Rima-di, however, nodded knowingly, murmuring, "Rini... I think I understand now."

Arunav stepped in, steadying the moment. He explained, "These eight colours symbolize the LGBTQ+ community. The name 'Gilbert' refers to Gilbert Baker, the activist who designed the rainbow flag as a symbol of pride and inclusion. This gift was not random—it was meant to honour Rini's truth. Our Rini does not just support the LGBT community—she belongs to it. She is a lesbian, by her preference."

The revelation sent ripples across the room. Zorika's eyes widened; in her community, such matters were taboo and never spoken aloud. Yet the surprise quickly gave way to curiosity, and then quiet acceptance. One by one, reactions emerged—each surprisingly warm, affirming. Rima-di broke the pause, recalling, "Do you all remember last year's Bihu fest, when we collected funds for 'Cultural Vikash Sangh' to support poor families? I noticed how close Rini was with her roommate, Bidisha. But I never thought in that direction, and we never talked about it."

Rini wiped her eyes again and nodded. "Yes, everyone, Bidisha and I... we share that bond. I was afraid all my life to tell anyone. Even with you, my family of friends, I hesitated. It wasn't because I didn't trust you. It was because of fear—fear of being judged, fear of being misunderstood, fear of losing the respect I found in you all. And most importantly to safeguard 'Bidisha'..." She paused, sipping the water Meghali handed her, before continuing. "It was only Arunav who discovered the truth back in December 2005, during Christmas."

Ananya's eyes widened. "Wait, that picnic to Lower Assam—when we decided to celebrate our birthdays together in that picnic; and you skipped it! And you said you weren't well and went home to Shillong. Right?"

Rini nodded. "That was a lie. By then, Bidisha and I had discovered each other's orientation. We decided to keep it secret and spent the holidays outside Assam, away from familiar eyes. We went to Arunachal, to meet some LGBT friends there. But as always, Arunav being so caring for his friend, when he tried to call me at my home, my family told him I wasn't there. He reached out to Bidisha, pieced it together, and eventually confronted us. And when we came back after the new year celebration, we both met him first. We broke down and confessed everything. We didn't know whether it was god's signal or something else, we felt that Arunav was the only one whom we can rely and happily express our situation. So myself and Bidisha cried out loud in front of him and we expressed all our feelings, about our relationship, about our hardship every day's struggle to hide our emotions, our pain. Arunav had not only accepted us with great grace, he decided to protect us in all corners and all possible ways. In fact, he had helped us many times in raising fund for our LGBT community team that we created. Though his vast network of friends from all corners, he helped us a lot understanding the international development in LGBT community. He often received information in email from his foreign friends, and we shared a great level of camaraderie".

She further added, "thus instead of judgment, Arunav gave us acceptance. He promised to keep this secret every way possible–always guiding us with quiet strength."

Niloy frowned slightly, asking, "But why didn't you tell us earlier? Haven't we been like a family these past three years? No trust?"

Before Rini could answer, Rima-di stepped in, protective and firm. "No, Niloy, it's not about trust. Rini is one of the strongest people here. She's lived alone, far from family, carrying this weight in silence. For teenagers and young adults like you all, who were still growing into life, it's not easy to reveal something so deeply personal. It takes courage–and tonight, she found it."

Ananya added, her voice soft but resolute, "And let's not forget Arunav. He kept her truth safe, respected her, and helped her in ways we never even knew. That's the mark of true friendship and maturity. We really respect you both".

Just then, Niloy suddenly shouted from the kitchen, "Guys, my pakodas! They're burning!" Laughter broke the tension as Meghali rushed in to save the snack. She called out cheerfully, "Alright everyone, tea's ready–it's time to celebrate our Rini."

Rini, still wiping tears, was lifted into a hug by Rima-di, Ananya, and Ron. In a spontaneous cheer, the group raised their voices together: "Waooo girl, you already have wings–now fly high in your sky!" Arunav added gently, "Yes, and this sky isn't just blue–it's painted in all eight shades, welcoming you to soar higher and higher."

The relief on Rini's face was unmistakable. What had begun as a burden she carried in silence ended in liberation, wrapped in acceptance and love. The room pulsed with dignity, pride, and affection, as all seven friends looked at her with even more respect than before. In that moment, their circle of friendship deepened, proving once again that true bonds thrive in truth and compassion.

Chapter 13:
Restless Currents - Continuing revelation

The hot pakodas and the sweet steam of chai had gently smoothed the edges of the late evening. Soft chatter filled the room again, and Rini's revelation had transformed into a warm celebration rather than a tense confession. Yet beneath the surface merriment, another current of restlessness had been building – Ron fidgeted more than usual, his phone buzzing at intervals he couldn't quite ignore.

Niloy, who had an eye for small changes in people's demeanours, watched him for a beat and then teased, "Ron babu, are you cooking up a new skit in real life or is there something else being cooked that we don't know?" Meghali, catching the nervous energy, ribbed him playfully: "Yes, yes–Ron is in a different grove today. Kya baat hai, bhai?"

To deflect the attention, Ron stuffed a few pakodas hurriedly into his mouth and muttered, "Coming, coming–wait a minute," then slipped toward the washroom, phone was tucked into the table when he rushed like a restless bird. Moments later, the washroom's door closed behind him. The yellow glow of the mobile screen flashed faintly in the hallway and Zorika, curious as ever, leaned over and read the incoming call: "Ahana Ma'am (Sr. Batch)".

The name struck something in everyone–an unfamiliar gravity, a hint of complexity. Ron, returning breathless, snatched the phone from Zorika. "Ahana ma'am?" Zorika laughed nervously, running to Rima-di for cover, whispering, "Who is this Ahana Ma'am? Why is she calling late?" Meghali chimed in, playfully, "Late night calls from a lady, Ron? Spill the tea, man!" Niloy, unable to hold back his blunt curiosity, leaned in and said in a tone that was half laughter and half suspicion, "Ron babu, something's cooking–bolo bhai, kya scene hai?"

Arunav's mind drifted for a moment, connecting dots. Ahana... Ahana... he thought. He had seen the name before–at Ron's studio–a poised woman who had come to enrol in Ron's classes. A memory surfaced: a rehearsing evening when Ron had shown him a flyer of new students. Hadn't one of them introduced herself as Ahana? He quietly wondered.

Back in the kitchen, as the kettle hissed and Niloy tended the frying pan, Zorika absentmindedly toppled a cup, splashing a little tea onto Ron's hand as he passed. A spark of anger flickered across his face, but it vanished almost as quickly as the steam. He took a deep breath and, somehow steadier, began to speak. "Guys... it's a little complicated," he admitted, sitting down with all the theatrical gravity he could muster. "I'm worried. I'm confused... and I don't want to hurt anyone."

Ananya, half-smile on her face, teased, "Ron, you and worry? They don't co-exist. Out with it–what happened?"

He closed his eyes for a second, fingers worrying the rim of his cup. The room slowed, as if the sound had been muffled so everyone could fit around the small, fragile thing he was about to lay down. Arunav watched him–he noticed the small habit Ron had of aligning his thumbs when he was about to tell the truth, a nervous ritual Ron never had time to perform onstage. Arunav felt the familiar, quiet impulse to order the chaos: listen, collect facts, sift emotion from detail. It was how he moved through problems, whether organizing a community workshop or keeping his own life tidy.

Ron started now saying "There's a woman–Ahana Gupta. She's older by 4 years to me, she enrolled at my studio about three months back, learning drama and some performance art. She's engaged–her fiancé is in Bengaluru, a banker. It was a professional relationship at first, but lately she's been sharing things... personal things. She told me she's not happy with her engagement and wants to escape the wedding. She needs a freedom with a creative career, that she discovered in my studio. Now–she says she loves me, loves this life full of creativity. And in fear that all these will vanish after her married life gets started."

Everyone was surprised as Ron is generally not into relationships. Ron then resumed "Ahana called today, again and again," Ron began. "She–she said she needs to talk. About something serious. About... well, about me, maybe." His voice cracked on the last word, and he tried to laugh it off. "I–last month, there was this night when we were returning from North Guwahati event. Ahana and my other teammates were there in that skit. She was upset. I stayed with her while she calmed down. She expressed her feeling for me. And I don't–" He stopped.

The group leaned forward because when Ron stopped, it meant he could not fix what was started alone. Niloy swore softly. "So you're saying– you guys hooked up? And now she's... pregnant," Niloy finished.

Continuing the Chapter:

Ron's laugh evaporated somewhere between the kettle's hiss and the clink of spoons. Then, with a voice that somehow managed to be both loud and fragile, he cut through the hum of the room. "Aree no baba, not pregnant and all," he began, throwing his hands up as if warding off a ridiculous suggestion. "She has been expressing strong disagreement with the current relationship and–" his words stumbled for a moment– "and over the last two months she has developed feelings for me. She says she can't leave, also she is stuck with the engagement she did."

The circle tightened. Arunav watched Ron closely; the kitchen light carved hollows under Ron's cheekbones that weren't usually there. Arunav asked the question that had been circling in his mind since Zorika read the name off the screen. "Ron, is she the same one I met at your studio that day?"

Ron nodded. In Arunav's memory the woman was poised and quiet on the edge of the rehearsal space, the kind of person who watched first and then spoke–the sort who made a room pause. "She looks pretty, quite graceful. But she is non-Assamese, I guess," Arunav added, more to himself than to anyone else.

"Yes," Ron said. "Her father–he's an Assamese Marwari. But she was born and brought up in Tezpur. They shifted here last year when her father expanded their business in Guwahati."

Meghali, who had the knack for cutting to the practical heart of things, asked bluntly, "So what's the problem? Don't you love her? Or is it the fear of commitment?"

Ron's hands found a pakoda as though they needed something tangible to hold on to. "No, Megha. It's not about liking. She's good in every way. But I'm not prepared." His voice grew steadier as he spoke, the theatricality dropping away to expose the real edge beneath. "I told Arunav many times–this happens. When we rehearse together, people get close. It's natural. But I can't get deviated from my goals."

Zorika's eyes widened. "How will a relationship deviate you from your goals? When love comes, we should embrace it."

Ron looked at her and then at Arunav. He seemed to collect the room with his gaze and lay a truth down, slow and soft. "After I lost my father in the first year of college... everything shifted. I lost a year of study. My mother–she struggled. My sister's dream is to become a pilot. We've had financial stress–there were liabilities my father left behind. That's why I had to start the Creative Studio here in Guwahati." He swallowed. "This studio is not just my art space. It's my livelihood. Every month I put money into an account for my sister, and another portion into a joint account for my mother and me. It's responsibility. I want to take this studio national—go to Mumbai, assist directors, climb up—so my sister's dream can be supported fully and my mother can have some peace."

Arunav felt something tighten in his chest, an old, familiar tilt of respect. He remembered the day when the visiting card that Ron had pressed into his hand at the very first meet in the bookfair in 2004; and then he remembered the day he first walked into Ron's studio: the earnestness in the way he described scenes and characters, the little diary that had perched by the visitor's stool—its pages closed but present like a folded promise. Arunav had never opened it. He had respected that boundary, but he'd also filed it away in the part of his mind meant for maps of people—where grief often lived beside ambition.

"Yes man," Arunav said now, softly, "I know this. When we first met, you showed me the studio. We had long talks, creative tasks... and I noticed that diary near the sitting area. I didn't go through it—didn't think to pry. But I always thought—Ron hides a lot beneath his creativity. He carries grief, yes, but also a long list of dreams."

Ron's nod was almost imperceptible; conviction steadied him. He went on, words coming out in a rush now as if he had been building to the confession for months. "It all goes into that account. I cannot afford to split my time. A relationship needs time—and time will divide my concentration. I'm not ready to give that up." His jaw clenched. "And this—Ahana—she's in true love with me. It developed organically. She's sensitive. She's already struggling to come out of an existing engagement. Any blunt no from me would hurt her. I'm afraid my humble 'no' will wreck her."

Rima-di, whose voice had been quiet until now, leaned forward and said what many of them were thinking aloud: "Yes, Ron. I second you. It is not easy to be in a relationship and still keep the freedom to create."

Garima, who had been uncharacteristically silent, met their eyes for a flicker of a second— a look that carried an unreadable weight. For a breath it felt as if she was waging her own small battle, a private map of compromises and compromises withheld. But the group's attention shifted away almost immediately; the room wanted to solve Ron's problem, not pry at Garima's.

Ron's fingers tightened around his cup. The smallness of the kettle's whistle, the occasional drip from the sink, the muted laughter in the next room—everything felt magnified. "I'm helpless," he said. "She needs an answer. She wants clarity because—" he glanced at Arunav "—she said her fiancé is coming next week. She wants to decide before that."

That line landed with a different kind of gravity. Arunav saw Ahana as a person with a life entangled in promises and obligations, not a mere obstacle to Ron's plan. He imagined her sitting alone that night, the same phone light cutting across her face, wrestling with a choice that would fracture two lives.

Arunav reached over and put his arm on Ron's shoulder in a brotherly gesture—simple, grounding. "Bro, don't worry," he said. "We'll sort this out. We'll sit together with Ahana. We'll work out how to tell her—gently, honestly. We won't let anyone be broken without mercy."

At that moment the phone buzzed again— insistent and small. Ron's face betrayed it: part dread, part obligation. He fumbled with the device, thumb hovering.

"Pick it up," Arunav said, quietly. "Take it into the other room. Speak softly."

Ron stood, shoulders tight, and walked away from the table, phone pressed to his ear. The yellow halo of the screen traced his profile for a heartbeat, then he slipped through the doorway and the kitchen's noise swallowed his steps.

The rest of them fell into motion without a word—chairs scooted in, cups were set down, a plan forming in the quiet cohort of friends. Arunav took a breath and, without dramatics, began to lay out what they could say, how they could frame it so Ahana would feel seen and not betrayed. They would be kind. They would be honest. They would try to make room for everyone's dignity.

Beyond the thin wall, Ron's voice softened; a muffled syllable reached them and then stopped. The kettle hissed, the last of the pakodas cooled on their plate. There were suspended breaths–the call, the choice, the careful promise of a small band of friends preparing to mediate a fragile heart.

Chapter 14 –
The Photograph and the Pause

Ron's footsteps receded into the other room and the kitchen's hum folded around them like a held breath. The small cluster at the table drew inwards, an orbit tightening to listen. Arunav folded his hands on the tabletop as if to steady the plan they were sketching, but before anyone could put words to policy or kindness, Garima – Rima-di to everyone, always the quiet centre – cleared her throat and offered, hesitantly, "I'd like to say something."

Her voice was low, uneven at first, as if she were sorting through an old cupboard and finding more than she expected. The group shifted; Niloy and Arunav exchanged a glance that said they had noticed a change in her for some time but had not pressed. Meghali's expression softened in that particular way she had when she guessed at a secret without needing proof. Ananya leaned forward, fingers hovering near her cup. Zorika watched with the wide-eyed curiosity of someone still learning how the world stored its larger hurts. Rini, unusually relaxed tonight, squeezed Zorika's hand like an anchor before slipping away for a quick call to Bidisha – a small ritual of consolation – then returned, cheeks flushed from conversation.

Garima began slowly, choosing each sentence as if it were a careful stitch. "Love is essential," she said, surprising the room with the conviction of it. "We need it. But sometimes–when time or situation is wrong–love can struggle. When that is the case, it's kinder to part than to cling and make both people smaller."

Her words landed not as doctrine but as something lived. Meghali's eyes sharpened in recognition. Ananya's mouth made the ghost of a smile, as if she had suspected a private rehearsal of these lines for years. Niloy and Arunav both felt the air densify, a sense that Garima was carrying an unspooled parcel and that it might be time to open it.

"Is there... something you want to tell us?" Arunav asked, careful. His voice held their usual warmth, the steady assurance of someone who did not flinch from other people's fragility.

Garima's fingers trembled the slightest when she reached into her drawer. From inside she produced a notebook – the kind with rounded corners and a spine softened by time. She flipped it open with reverence, and the others saw pages of neat handwriting and little pressed petals. From between the pages she drew an old photograph.

The photo was the kind that belongs in a time that remembers itself fondly: a group of young men and women on a sunlit college lawn, laughter trapped mid-frame. Garima stood out – not ostentatiously, but with a calm charm that the camera adored. Next to her, a young man leaned forward, his posture casual but certain. Garima pointed to him.

"This is John Bungton," she said, and there was a tiny defiant lift in the way she pronounced the name. "This is my man."

For a moment the only sound was the kettle's faint hiss and the soft scrape of a chair as someone shifted. The late evening outside the window seemed to press closer, turning the kitchen into a small theatre where this admission played big and bright.

"Bungton da – from Delhi, right?" Arunav said then, with that pleased certainty that comes when a remembered name clicks into place. His tone carried a friendly poke; he'd been to Delhi enough to know the type.

Meghali's nod was small but meaningful. "Yes, Nav. Bungton da is Rima-di's love. They've been... a hidden thing." Her words fell into the circle like a dropped pebble, concentric and widening.

Garima's smile was not triumphant but wistful. She folded the photograph and let it rest on the table between them. "There's more," she said. She searched their faces one by one, not for sympathy but for permission, as if apologizing for having a wound that might not be neat. "Probably I never dared to tell this, being the elder here. I was afraid it would set a precedent for you all—wrong footsteps for young hearts."

Niloy's impatience peered through his concern. "More to it? Wrong precedent? Come on, Rima di – this is already a lot tonight with Rini and Ron. So please tell us all in detail. Rain is outside, thundering storm alike, Arunav's last meal here with us. So no one is leaving, we have enough time. Boliye please!"

At that, the kitchen filled with minor noises: spoons against saucers, a low exhale from Ananya, Zorika's small intake of breath as she tried to catch up with details, she had only half-sensed all evening. Rini, just back from the call with Bidisha, dropped into her chair as if settling back into safety. "Did I miss anything?" she asked, bright and slightly breathless. "Rima-di, start—what's your story?"

Garima's hand rested on the photograph as if grounding herself. Outside the thin partition where Ron spoke, a low murmur of his voice threaded through the wall – just fragments: "I... I can't hurt you," followed by a small, sharp inhale, then the muffled shaking of a breath. Now and then an unfinished sentence rode back: "Please... wait–" and then silence, the kind that feels like a held back tide. The call's cadence had the same rhythms as a decision being born – stops and starts, a hope that might still be renegotiated.

Inside the room, eyes met eyes. The lamps cast gentle circles; the table bore crumbs of pakoda and puddles of forgotten tea. Garima took another breath and, as if wading into deeper water, began to speak.

But before the first unravelling sentence could fall into the air, Arunav's calm voice offered again – a soft anchor: "We're with you, Rima-di. Say whatever you want. There's no judgement here."

The moment held like a poised hand – tender, expectant – as if the kitchen itself was leaning in. Garima's lips parted. The photograph waited on the table like evidence of a life that had been quietly kept. Somewhere beyond the wall, the other life – Ron's life – balanced on a ring of light and a single spoken word.

Rini, her curiosity edged with affection, leaned forward and murmured, "Please. Tell us."

And then suddenly there is power-cut, the conversation took a pause on that charged stillness: Garima, ready to unveil; friends, ready to receive; and Ron's conversation, threading through the night like a second story half-heard, half-known, promising consequences that would soon come to full voice.

Chapter 15 –
Candlelight Confessions

The lights blinked and then died–softly, as if the house itself had taken a long, tired breath. Ananya's voice cut through the sudden hush with a note of exasperation. "Come on–transformer is gone, it seems. This has happened three times this week."

Zorika padded to the cupboard and produced a candle, its small flame a stubborn, golden eye in the dark. She set it in the centre of the floor and everyone rearranged themselves into a loose circle, faces brightened by the flicker and shadow. The room felt smaller and somehow more honest under the candle's fragile rule: secrets looked easier to speak when no electric light could give them the polish of rehearsed performance.

Before words could settle, Ron appeared in the doorway, silhouette sharp against the hallway. Arunav's face softened. “All sorted, boy?” he asked. Meghali followed, voice threaded with concern, “Ron, hope things are manageable and the worry is less now.”

“It seems so,” Ron said, quietly. “But I’ll really need your help to sort this out. But not now, it’ll be late for her at home—she stays with her parents. So... can we call her in the morning?” His fingers twisted the phone in a nervous rhythm.

Garima was quick to answer. “Why not, Ron? In fact, let’s invite her for breakfast. We’re not going to sleep till late morning anyway and Arunav will leave before noon tomorrow.” The suggestion landed like a promise. It was Saturday morning after all—no one had to be anywhere early. Voices rose in easy agreement; Ron agreed to drop her an SMS.

He hesitated, then offered, a smile trying to make itself useful, “I know I missed a lot maybe, but let me get into your conversation.”

Rini nudged him with a grin. “No man, you’re spot on. We’re about to meet our to-be Jiju.” Laughter warmed the circle—light, saving, ordinary.

Garima’s face shifted then—something between joy and an exhale. She sat up a little straighter and, with a sudden hush that made everyone tilt forward, said, “Guys—John is not my boyfriend. He is my husband.”

The sentence landed and the room stilled, as if the candle flame itself had paused. Shock rippled through them: eyebrows rose, cups stilled in mid-air, and a hundred questions fluttered up unasked. If she was married, why the distance? Why the secrecy? Arunav's mind reached back, linking a name he'd heard in Delhi to the photograph Rima-di had shown earlier.

His memory unspooled for a moment, and he began, almost by reflex, to bridge past and present. "I remember meeting Bungton da in Delhi," he said. "I met him through work—back when I was part of that digital literacy campaign, Ebiz Education Venture." The circle listened; his voice carried the kind of easy authority that comes from lived involvement.

Arunav told them how, in early 2005, after shifting to a PG near Ulubari, he'd been drawn into a chain-marketing network that doubled as a social cause—digital literacy for underprivileged students. They all knew about this Ebiz initiative that Arunav promoted, in fact Ron and Dhruv also joined this for some time. He narrated that two senior guys had been establishing that network's legs in the Northeast and Arunav, always socially active, had joined. With a head for organizing, he had quickly built a team of more than thirty people in his chain, each sign-up translating into free digital education—books and internet-café access—for three underprivileged students. As part of the global initiative, he'd travelled to Amritsar, Faridabad, and Pune; the work had a pulse and a purpose.

"One of the times I was in Delhi last year," Arunav went on, the past opening like a window, "Rima-di asked me to meet and stay with John Bungton—he was helpful, hospitable. He and his roommates hosted me and other colleagues for a couple of days. Bungton da was decent, earnest—Delhi types who still had room for idealistic work." He gave a small, affectionate shrug. "We kept in touch. I always liked how the Ebiz thing folded real help into a network. I stepped back from the marketing leg during college's third year—I had to—time became scarce. But some people and causes stay with you."

The recollection filled the circle in gentle detail, making the jumble of Garima's revelation and Arunav's memory cohere into a larger picture. Garima, who had been watching the faces around her like a woman re-checking weather before stepping out, nodded and then spoke again—her voice steady and full of a kind of remembered conviction.

"Yes," she said. "We were in deep love. Right after college we lived together in Guwahati and decided to get married soon. But when we told our families... it exploded." She let the word hang, dry and accurate. "I'm Garima Ahmed—Hindu-Muslim by family—and John is Christian from Manipur. The opposition came from every corner. People said we were wrong for each other.

We were young, stubborn, and a little naive perhaps, but the love was not something we could just switch off."

They listened like students of human weather–watchful, compassionate. Rini and Zorika had questions clustered like lightning about to leap; Meghali and Ananya absorbed the tale with a slower, reflective curiosity, the kind that learns from a sister's wound. They knew about John somewhat in between, but not like this real story. Then Niloy's attention sat somewhere between protective and practical.

Garima continued: "We decided to marry under the law. It was quick, a small court ceremony–something that felt like staking a claim in a world that had tried to deny us. John went to Delhi for his MBA and then for a job. I stayed here to finish my law practice. Our plan: work, save, and once we were stable, go abroad–UK–start life anew where family objections would matter less."

The story unfolded like a map of compromises they had already made. Distance, it became clear, had not meant abandonment. It had been a strategy: protect the relationship, shield it from the immediate social pressure, and build a future that would demand acceptance rather than plead for it.

Meghali, connecting dots she had only half-seen, smiled wryly. "Ah–no wonder you always select Delhi for your conferences; I can relate now." Garima's smile was small, private. "Honestly, we trusted each other. We played the conference and work cards because our families don't know the truth. They think we broke up after the opposition. John comes to Guwahati every six months when he can. That's how we've stayed together—long-distance, in secrecy, surviving on the small returns of visits and letters."

Niloy's practical voice asked what they were all thinking. "So—how long can you hide this? His family? Your family? Won't the truth come out?"

A shadow crossed Garima's face. She answered softly, the next sentence careful as a footstep on glass: "We've gone through a lot, Niloy. Early on I even got pregnant. We thought the child would be our anchor. But we had to abort realizing the unbearable pressure and turmoil we would face—both social and family. No one knows. We've borne it between us. We wait for financial stability—one day when we can leave, when distance removes the immediate family pressure, we will reveal everything. We hope that once we are physically away, with our finances sorted, the acceptance will be easier."

The confession reverberated in the candlelight. For a moment no one spoke. The air held grief and admiration in equal measure: grief for what had been lost, admiration for the endurance that had kept the marriage alive in the face of social storms.

As the night deepened and the candle burned lower, the kitchen felt less like a gossip space and more like an archive of lives–unpolished, honest records stacked between chai stains and pakoda crumbs. Each person drew a lesson into themselves: about love that refuses to die quietly, about strategy and survival, about the small cruelties of social expectations and the quiet heroism of those who persist anyway. Now Arunav realized Rima-di's dream "to study global law abroad and return to establish a law firm dedicated to social justice and women's rights". He uttered in mind "yes, it all makes sense". Huge respect and admiration for both Garima and John filled his heart.

Rini, shaken by sympathy and a new layer of understanding, reached for Garima's hand. Meghali's face had softened into a look of fierce respect. Zorika, who had only just begun to learn about adult compromises, watched like someone seeing a complex painting for the first time–colours she had not yet names for.

Outside, the night deepened. Ron's voice moved through the thin wall again–nearer now, more composed. Words slipped: "I think she understands... We'll speak in the morning." The cadence of resolution threaded through the room; there was a sense that decisions were being stitched across doors and phone lines, sewn by friends who had learned to keep each other.

Dinner was long over. The candle waned to a stubborn pool of light. Stillness arrived not as emptiness but like a well-earned pause—everyone presents, held by the gravity of Garima's story and the small, private oaths of courage and patience it revealed. Lessons had been given without sermon: trust, endurance, the high cost of secrecy, and the quiet bravery of choosing each other every day.

The candle was almost melted with the image of the circle—faces drawn soft by the flame, the photograph folded upon the table like a small artifact of rebellion—while beyond the wall two lives considered the shape of the next morning: a breakfast invitation, a delicate conversation, and the hopeful plan to hold one another steady through whatever came next.

Chapter 16 –
Midnight Kitchens and Quiet Walks

The confession had thinned the air, but it did not still it. Garima rose as if a small domestic rebellion would be the antidote to heavy hearts. "Ron, come help me with the rotis," she said, half-teasing, half-commanding. The invitation landed like a gentle order—practical, grounding. Ron blinked, surprised out of his self-made fog, then followed her into the kitchen with an obedient smile.

Meghali and Arunav claimed the pan for egg-curry without ceremony, setting out the onions, tomatoes and spices with efficient, comfortable movements. Niloy stood, stretching, then volunteered to check the Dhaba on the corner for tandoori leg pieces. "It's almost eleven, but the Dhaba might still have some. I am going to check?" he was about to leave. Rini hopped up without hesitation: "wait, I'll come with you. I need the walk."

Zorika moved through the house gathering cups and cushions, and as she arranged them she began to hum a tune from her village–an easy, flowing melody in a language that felt new to most of them. The sound was bright and unpretentious; it stitched the room back together. Ananya joined in with a soft hum of her own, and soon two unfamiliar phrases braided into a lullaby-like chorus that made everyone softer around the edges. Even those who didn't understand the words found their shoulders loosen.

The candle had consumed an hour's worth of light when the mains blinked back to life. Power restored. Lamps reasserted themselves with a quiet click; the room filled and everyone breathed as if waking, a small cheer passing through as phones relit and the mundane comfort of electricity returned like a small mercy.

Arunav's phone chimed. A message from Dhruv lit the screen: "Nav, our event will be over by 3 am, it is going as great success. We missed you. We will leave from here by morning, see you by afternoon." Arunav typed back, the habitual warmth of the reply already forming: "Great to know guys, drive safe, see you soon."

The message tugged him briefly into the world beyond the kitchen–the other friendships and commitments that braided through his life. He felt that familiar swell of affection and a little pang for the goodbyes that were always around the corner. He chose memory over melancholy and, with a small smile, returned to the kitchen.

Eggs bubbled in a half-simmering bath while Meghali chopped onions with the kind of rhythm that made even tears look purposeful. Arunav—true to his ritual—began sending goodnight SMSs. It had not always been easy: in the early days, he joked, the money for messages was scarce, and BSNL's free packs were a lifeline. He'd kept that habit when networks multiplied; the messages were small talismans—quotes, silly lines, a short note of affection—tokens that knit people together from a distance.

Out on the street Niloy and Rini walked side by side, the tandoori glow from the City Dhaba windows painting them warm. The city at night had a kinder face after the showers: chai vendors still brewing, a few late-night customers, the smell of frying oil and spices crossing the air.

"So how was Bidisha?" Niloy asked casually, though his eyes suggested he wanted every small detail.

Rini laughed softly, fingers brushing the sleeve of her shirt as if smoothing a memory. "It was... different," she said. "I was terrified at first. Bidisha is older, very sure of herself, an anchor. She helped me see parts of myself I had been running from." She tucked a stray hair behind her ear. "We met at that book outlet in Panbazar—remember? I had the copy of my draft and she spoke for ten minutes about the way I wrote a scene. I thought she was being kind, but she had... depth. She later invited me to a reading group, followed by wall painting. That became our small world."

Niloy listened, the streetlight catching the curve of his face. "And now?"

"Now I'm not afraid," Rini said simply. "We've promised small things. She's not flashy with words, but she's steady. She wanted to come with me tonight because she wanted to meet my people but we were not prepared. Honestly —I did not know that I would be able to say it all. Thanks to Arunav, his magical gift not only consoled me but got me the platform to tell my reality in front of you all. Thanks to you all, tonight I felt free. I'm not carrying the old fear anymore." Her voice was quiet, but it carried an unburdened joy.

The Dhaba yielded their tandoori legs with a friendly, greasy flourish. The vendor smiled at their chatter and packed the meat in foil. Back at the house the aroma met them at the doorway—charred spices, garlic notes, the smell of a feast improvised—enough to pull a laugh from even the most solemn face.

In the kitchen, rotis were spun and slapped on the hot tawa. Garima moved with a practiced ease–knead, rest, pat, and flip–her hands carrying the history of many kitchens. Ron watched, asking little questions as he helped, his curiosity practical and earnest. "How do you keep the rotis soft?" he asked. Garima answered with small, exact instructions: the right amount of water, the patience to roll without squeezing, the secret puff technique she used to coax air under the dough. Her hands, in the half-light, looked like the map of a life that had learned to make room for small miracles.

Their conversation folded from cooking techniques to larger stitches of meaning. Ron's voice, at first faltering, grew steadier as he unloaded the knot of his confusion about Ahana.

"She says she can't leave," he repeated, "and she wants an answer before her fiancé arrives next week. I don't know how to say no without hurting her."

Garima wiped her palms, then leaned against the counter and looked at him with that same steady warmth he'd seen before–a mix of tenderness and hard-won clarity. "Ron," she said gently, "love should be honest. But being honest doesn't mean obliterating someone. You don't owe her a story you don't want to be in."

He frowned. "What if she gets destroyed? She's fragile."

"Then you have to be kinder," Garima said. "Tell her before anything is set. Don't invent a reason—your truth is enough. Say you care, but you cannot give her what she needs now. Don't promise what you can't deliver, and don't ghost her. If she's already tied to an engagement, you need to be particularly gentle. Offer her the chance to talk, to ask questions, to understand why. And if she wants space, give it. Sometimes the noblest thing is to offer clarity, even if it hurts."

Ron opened his mouth, then shut it, digesting the counsel like a meal. "Will that be selfish?" he asked.

"Not selfish—responsible," Garima corrected. "Selfish would be to let her hope because you are too afraid to break it gently. Also remember: your responsibility to your family and your dreams is valid. Love doesn't always mean choosing the same timeline. You can love a person and still refuse an arrangement that will derail both of you."

He nodded, a small, relieved motion, as if a taut string had loosened. Garima continued, softer now, "And be honest with your friends. We will sit with you tomorrow morning. If you want, make it a confronting meeting, so she doesn't feel blindsided by a private 'no'. We can help you frame it—words that show respect rather than rejection."

Ron's eyes flicked toward the door where he could hear fragments of his own muffled conversation from earlier—another life being negotiated. "I... I think I can do that," he murmured. "...Thank you."

Niloy and Rini arrived with the aromatic tandoori in hand. Meanwhile, Meghali and Arunav finished the egg-curry with a flourish—spices blooming, mustard seed popping, the fragrance slipping through the house like an invitation. They plated the food, brought hot rotis fresh off the tawa, and set the tandoori pieces on a small platter as if making a banquet fit for reconciliation.

They ate around the low table, hands and fingers occasionally reaching for pickle and spice, laughter threading through stories about students and missed buses and ridiculous auditions. The heaviness of earlier hours had softened: confession had not broken them but folded them tighter together.

Outside, the night kept its quiet. Inside, the clatter of plates and the soft exchange of confidences settled into something near domestic grace—people who forgave each other's human mess and tasted together the ordinary comforts of food, light, and company.

The midnight party was over almost –a kitchen alive with flame and talk, a circle of friends nourished by the food and by small truths, Ron steadier for advice from a woman who had loved and endured, Rini and Niloy returning with tandoori legs and stories, and Arunav sending one more goodnight SMS into the city before switching off his phone and letting the house fall gently into a hush of sleep.

Before they call it a night and take some naps, Ron hugged Arunav with mix of joy and emotion. And he admitted "it was not just a farewell bro, your last day here made it special for all of us. We all found new meanings in life, new perspectives". Then Ananya added "Yes guys, our team, this family has found true name today as we confirmed earlier "The Purples"...!". Then Meghali uttered with joy "Yes yes, The purples, like the name reflects, we discovered a new precious colour within ourselves. That's lifelong friendship."

Purple is the colour of mixtures – blue's calm braided with red's fire, and so it fits them: a circle that holds steadiness and passion in equal measure. Calling themselves "The Purples" became a small emblem of who they were tonight – a twilight band where secrets and laughter sit side by side, where grief and hope are allowed the same soft light. Purple is royal without arrogance, mysterious without menace; it suggests resilience, creativity and the courage to keep faith when things get complicated. Tonight, they practiced all of that – being patient (blue), being brave (red), and turning bruises into petals that don't hide but bloom. In that single name was their promise: to stay loyal when the world demanded easy choices, to listen when hearts spoke in half-words, and to keep returning to each other like dusk returning to the city. It's familiar, deep, and quietly insistently beautiful.

Everyone hugged each other, a joy of being together, being bonded filled the room.

Arunav cried, while Zorika was already full of tears, Rini was overwhelmed with all these gestures.

As the night was about to get absorbed into the hopeful morning lights which was under formation, another soft jamming session from Rini with her guitar made the night even more beautiful.

Chapter 17 –
Puri, Prayers, and Practical Hearts

"Good morning, Purples!" Zorika's voice floated through the room like a bright ribbon of sound. She was up before everyone, as she usually was, and the spicy steam of ginger tea followed her footsteps. The low table was a scatter of cushions and the floor still wore last night's small chaos: pillows in a soft tumble, scarves draped over chairs, and the long carpet pressed down in the places where they had slept. The hall had become a communal bed; the whole household looked like a gentle, improvised nest.

One by one they rose, moved through their small morning rituals, and slipped into the bathroom in a slow, easy procession. The house creaked awake with them–showers running, towels thudding gently, the occasional laugh from the veranda. When Garima and

Ananya finished folding their saris, kurtas, and sari-blouses, there came a knock at the door and down from the second-floor landed the loving landlord aunty, her palms full of a small tin of homemade cookies and a smile that had never learned to be anything but generous.

"For you, beta," she said, offering the tin to Garima and the others. She peered about at the scattered pillows and the young faces bright with the glow of the night. "What's the occasion? Bit of a party? You youngsters always make this place lively." Garima's cheeks warmed.

"It's a small farewell," Garima answered. "Arunav leaves tonight for higher studies."

The old aunt's face lit like someone who had tracked each child's life as if tending a garden. "Where is Arunav? Let me bless him." Arunav emerged from the room at that precise moment, hair still damp, wiping his feet before stepping down. He cupped the aunt's hand and, with the respectful gesture he often reserved for elders, touched her feet. The old woman's blessing fell on him in simple, earnest words.

"All the best, beta. You will prosper in life." She looked at the group with a fond appraisal and added, voice softening as if naming a truth she'd kept for years, "You all share such nice bonds. We never felt disturbed by your visits. In fact, your maturity in managing the house makes us very proud. God bless you all." She waved, and her footsteps retreated up the stairs, leaving a warmth that stayed with them.

Arunav stood a little straighter from that blessing, the weight of future and hope suddenly lighter. He tasted it—a small surety that the journey ahead might be hard but also fruitful.

A message blinked on Ron's phone; he had sent Ahana the SMS the night before and, while his reply had been hesitant then – "Maybe, will see if I can come"—this morning came a decisive note: "Good morning, Ron, I will be there. Send me the address." Relief and nervousness threaded his smile as he read it aloud, and the room tightened into practical motion.

Arunav nudged Rini with a conspiratorial grin. "Rini—why don't you invite Bidisha too? It will be good to have her here before I go."

Meghali chimed in, "Yes, yes—she's part of us now; bring her." Rini nodded and, with a small flutter in her voice, called Bidisha who happily agreed.

Breakfast took shape like a ritual: puris puffing golden on the tawa, sabji simmering with soft potatoes and spices, Ananya stirring a fragrant kheer, Zorika and Garima moving together like a practiced duet. Meghali, with her special milk tea—strong, frothy, and a touch of cardamom—poured it into waiting cups; steam drew small halos above their faces, and the house smelled of cumin and fried dough and cardamom, the scent of common celebrations.

When Ahana arrived, Ron went down the lane to meet her at the gate. She stepped in with a modest, composed elegance—a woman slightly older than most of them but younger than Garima, carried in with a poise that balanced confidence and a little tension. Everyone greeted her with that mix of curiosity and kindness that defined The Purples. Arunav's face was a familiar, calming presence for her, and early on she opened with a small confession that dismantled a corner of formality.

"I think I met you at Ron's studio," she said, looking at Arunav. The conversation broke into easy warmth after that—someone reminisced, someone asked about classes, someone cracked a joke about last night's pakodas—and the house grew softer with laughter. Yet in the space between the jokes, Ahana and Ron's faces kept returning to a quieter line; her eyes sometimes searched his as if looking for a final certainty, his replies small and careful.

Garima, who had a steadying way, poured herself a cup of tea and set it down with deliberate slowness. She addressed Ahana gently, beginning not with theory but with a small story—a domestic reference from the earlier night meant to set the direction: "We all had a long conversation last night about how love sometimes comes when life isn't ready. It doesn't make either person a villain; it simply asks for clarity."

Ahana listened. Her hands folded around her cup like someone anchoring herself. The food drew the group together and plates filled; the puris were light and the sabji bright–comfort food that loosened words. Conversation unfurled–small talk, stories of childhood, memories of the studio–then Garima threaded the talk toward the knot at the centre.

She did it with care: naming the dignity of feeling, and the dignity of promises. "We value love here," Garima said, looking at Ahana with an openness that asked no immediate decision. "But we also believe that when others' futures are on the line, we owe them an honest, measured thought. Love is not only about the current pulse; it is about responsibility."

Ahana's reply was steady, grown-up in the way of someone who had been thinking hard nights through. "I got confused," she said, voice low. "I thought I had to follow my heart, and I confess I leaned on Ron because he gave me attention and kindness at a time I needed it. My fiancé–he is kind and unaware. I didn't want to hurt him either."

The room listened as if listening were the first step in a respectful act. Ananya's eyes were wet with small comprehension; Meghali's posture had the calm of someone reconciling two facts at once. Niloy and Rini sat across, their hands on their cups, watching the exchange with a mix of protection and curiosity.

Ron spoke, voice deliberate. "I never wanted to ask her to break anything," he said. "I was trying not to hurt. But I was also scared of what saying 'no' might do to her—I thought my silence would be softer."

Garima leaned in. "Silence becomes a sword if left long enough. Ahana, you have a decision. But the kindest route is to tell the truth to all involved. If you need time to think with your fiancé—take it. Don't make sudden, unanchored choices. Give them both the gift of honesty."

One by one, they offered practical counsel without pressure: let Ahana speak to her fiancé, consider counselling, avoid rash moves, and ensure that any choice respects everyone's dignity. Arunav, who had always been pragmatic about social ties and responsibilities, suggested a structured pause—meet with the fiancé with a mediator if needed, or at least allow time for everyone to process.

Under the umbrella of this counsel, Ahana inhaled, then nodded. "I think the right thing is to talk to him properly," she said. "I need to see if my feelings are just a refuge in my confusion or something that can withstand honesty. I won't ask him to break his promise without a real reason." Her voice showed resolution—not the sudden fervour of infatuation, but the steadier warmth of someone making a grown choice.

Relief washed across Ron's face. It was neither triumph nor defeat; it was a soft easing of the chest. The group breathed with him. They'd hoped for clarity but not at the cost of someone else's life. The Purples had come together not to demand but to shepherd a better path.

Their breakfast wound down in that comfortable silencing–the kind that follows when things are decided with care. Bowls were emptied, plates stacked, and laughter returned to the small corners of the room. At the door, just as they were about to rise and clear the table, a presence was felt: Bidisha stood there, bag slung across her shoulder, her face framed in polite eagerness. She had come–on Rini's call–and at that precise moment the circle felt full again.

This morning phase closes on that gentle image: a table scattered with crumbs and cardamom in the air, a group of friends who had navigated an awkward, tender morning and arrived at a place of mutual respect. Ahana, upright and composed, had chosen truth and time; Ron had been granted a breathing space; Arunav carried a blessing that felt like ballast; Garima's quiet steadiness had held the conversation. And at the door, Bidisha's arrival hinted that new threads would be woven into The Purples' shared fabric–threads of friendship, possibility, and another story waiting to be told.

Chapter 18 –
New Threads in Purple

As soon as Bidisha stepped into the room, the tenuous thread between Ahana and Ron loosened into something gentler; with a small, friendly gesture their delicate exchange found its quiet close and the group melted into a new, warmer orbit. Rini beamed as she proudly introduced Bidisha to everyone – "This is Bidisha, my mate". Bidisha greeted the room "Hey–good morning, Purples!" while Ahana, a little out of the loop on the newcomer's backstory, the term Purples, she simply smiled and mingled with her for a few moments before excusing herself. Ron walked her to the gate where her car waited, their goodbye soft and composed, and then he turned back to a house that had already begun rearranging itself around a new face and another story.

Bidisha's arrival had broken whatever hush was left after Ahana left. She stepped inside with the easy calm of someone used to rooms full of strangers turning into friends. Rini glowed as she moved to introduce her, pride bright in every step. "Please meet Bidisha, meeting you all for first time," she said, chest warm and proud. Bidisha smiled, shook hands, exchanged small pleasantries, and the room folded her in as if she had always been meant to fit.

A quiet settled, then the house filled again with fresh, friendlier noise – plates, the clink of spoons, and Rini telling everyone one little proud anecdote after another about how she met Bidisha. Bidisha laughed and responded in kind; she was curious, warm, and in moments she spoke with a clarity that made people listen.

Breakfast turned into a slow Saturday that smelled of cardamom and comfort. Conversation spread like tea steam – light, sharing, and sometimes deep. The centre of the morning became Rini and Bidisha: stories, jokes, memories, and sudden, thoughtful pauses. At one point Bidisha gently steered the talk into LGBT topics, not as lecture but as friendly sharing. She explained with simple clarity: the difference between identity and orientation, the small battles of recognition, the pride and the practicalities of living openly or not. Rini – who carried pride like a new flag – added her experiences, blunt and brave: how small acts of acceptance had changed her world, how community and chosen family mattered. The group listened, asked questions, laughed, and learned; it was cheerful and informative, the kind of exchange that turned ignorance into empathy.

Mid-morning, Arunav's phone rang and the house answered in chorus. Dhruv, on loudspeaker with Dimppan, boomed in: "Hey guys, hope the evening was great and the morning brighter! We're bringing some jinda desi murga from the hills and smoked pork for our little champions." The speaker crackled merrily. Zorika's face lit up – she and Rini loved smoked meat by tradition – and the kitchen's energy doubled at the promise.

"Also, bring some cold desi bottles!" Ron hollered from the veranda, voice half playful, half pleading. He stopped short as he remembered the company: a sheepish, "ah–wait–never mind," and a grin. Rini called back, teasing: "Remember, additional guests now – and don't forget fresh pineapples from Jorabat junction!" The banter threaded through the lane into laughter, and someone shouted directions back to the car.

The day wore on with the comfortable mess of close friends. Clouds drifted over a lazy blue sky; sunlight found their faces in stripy patches. Arunav slipped away for a moment to call Mon, asking him to get some prints ready for the evening meeting – little things that would keep the next day tidy. He knew that this will be a busy with The Purples, so he already sent some important documents to Mon for him to help with prints. He was a man who planned: neat travel routes, travel tickets checked, a list of what his parents needed to pack. He insisted they fly from Dibrugarh rather than Guwahati – less travel, fewer connections, an easier beginning for their trip to Delhi. Even as his heart soaked up the last hours with The Purples, his mind flickered through checklists and confirmations. It was the kind of double-focus that had carried him this far: feeling everything deeply and also lining up practical steps for tomorrow.

Back inside, the house turned into a bright, noisy theatre. Dhruv and Dimppan arrived like a small, boisterous caravan, bearing parcels that smelled of smoke and spice. Plates were set, and the tandoori murga made a dramatic entrance; the smoked pork was wrapped and unwrapped like treasure for Zorika and Rini, they occasionally love to have smoked pork falls under their gathering or during fest too.

Meghali made a pot of chai thick enough to warm stubborn bones. A board game was set up on the low table – a quick, competitive round for anyone who loved small fights and loud cheers – while others drifted to the guitar for a little jam. Rini and Bidisha swapped songs and poems, the music soft and honest, the kind that turned afternoons into memory.

At one point everyone gathered to review again the gifts Arunav had brought last night – simple but so mindfully picked things, with lot of efforts visible in handmade outcomes, each carrying thoughts. They took turns trying to read the hidden meaning in each present, teasing one another about choices and intent. It was like everyone tried to see other's gift and try to interpret the deep meaning that each gift carry. Full of appreciation and respect rose into the room for Arunav, once again. They wanted to thank Arunav again, then everyone felt short of words against the gestural and heartfelt efforts displayed in those meaningful gifts.

As the afternoon became noisier and friendlier, someone turned the conversation back to the group's name. "The Purples," Meghali said, raising her cup like a toast. "We keep getting new colours in our mix." Bidisha smiled, the new thread in the weave, and Rini squeezed her hand in a silent welcome.

Arunav sat back and watched them: a small, messy, beautiful cluster of people who had come together for reasons both small and large. They argued about rules in the board game, laughed at a clumsy chorus, and paused to listen when someone played the chord that made the room breathe. The house felt lived-in and loved.

Arunav smiled with great dignity while his eyes aligned with Garima and then Ananya, with a soft, reflective voice in their minds: another member had joined the circle – Bidisha, whose presence brought fresh words and new light. The Purples had expanded, their shade deepening: still the same mix of calm and fire, and now with an added streak of bookish warmth and careful clarity. They were, as always, learning what it meant to be family by choice – a colour that kept growing richer the more threads they wove into it.

Chapter19 –
Sandwiches of Time

"Good noon, Purples..." Ananya's voice had barely finished before the question landed, practical and a little anxious. "So—what's the plan for lunch now?" Glances around the room betrayed the same thought: it was nearly noon, and time was scurrying toward Arunav's leave-with Dhruv and Dimppan at 3 pm.

"Yeah—plan quick," Meghali urged, "already thinking about what everyone in this eventful day would please. Nav will leave hungry otherwise."

Arunav waved them off with the calm of someone who had already arranged more than one surprise in his life. "Relax, girls. I think you all forgot. I told you guys three days ago—Saturday lunch is on me. I've have already placed order from O Tenga." The name drew a cheer: O Tenga, with its little map of Northeast flavours, was perfect. Zorika smiled and even expressed her joy with some line in her own native language. Arunav recalled "Yes – bamboo shoot rice and fish for Rima-di and Ananya, some surprising tribal dishes for Rini and Zorika, now also to be shared by our lovely Bidisha." He continued, "something buttery for our Niloy, the flavourful Thupka bowl for dear Megha and smoky treats to appease the visiting boys, including me & Ron !". Meghali clapped with joy as if she had not acknowledged him, but was so pleased with these amazing choices of food. Zorika, as always excited with her purity in smile, raised a hi-five with Rini and Bidisha.

But then there was a small practical hitch–home delivery from "O Tenga" was thin on weekend drivers. Also, home delivery of food was not a common practice in Guwahati that time, although 'O Tenga' offers that service. Dimppan volunteered instead: "I'll go pick it up." He shrugged as if it were nothing; the group accepted immediately. Arunav gave him the order reference so that it will be quick for him to pick up the food. Dimppan wasn't always around in this team–he remained engaged with his fitness, modelling assignments, a busy schedule–but he turned up when his cousin Zorika needed him or Dhruv and Arunav called him every time; and today that was enough.

As they waited, the room subtly conspired to make the last hours roomy and true. Dhruv and Dimppan were due to leave by three; Arunav's bag sat neat and zipped in the corner; yet few things to be settled as there is another small gathering awaited with Mon and his club-friends.

Arunav was a man who planned journeys like good stories: clear in the map, generous in the heart. So his travels along with his travel bags, some parcels that will be sent hometown, all were almost in order at his room. But he had to hand over the keys to his landlord after a little last cleaning swipes.

Then the mood shifted. The easy chatter folded into a soft stillness as everyone realized how thin time had become–how each minute now scattered like bright dust. Arunav stood up slowly, the way people do when they are going to say something true. "Guys," he began, voice steady but small, "these three years–what a chapter. I didn't know I would be so full of feelings today. I wrote a few lines in last few days. May I read them?"

He looked at each face in the circle, and in that look was the mild command of a man who trusted the people in front of him. Zorika's eyes shone first; a small tremor of memory leaked through her smile. Ananya's fingers tightened around her cup. Ron, Garima, Meghali, Niloy, Rini, Bidisha–each face softened into attention. Arunav took a breath and read.

"For dear Rini – who tuned a bookshop glance into a universe, an empty wall to a canvas of colours, a doorway; small brave steps that taught us how to stay. For the friend who learned to love steady, not loud: you teach us how small kindnesses hold whole world around.

For dear Zorika – whose songs stitch the room together like warm thread, her pen has magic that pour heart, who wakes at dawn to make tea as if morning were a promise: your voice made a thousand nights less lonely.

For Ron boy – who keeps two homes in his hands, the studio and the messy room; whose grit is a ledger of dreams for others, creativity is the blood flowing under his skin: you make art into duty and duty into wings. Salute !

For our Garima – our Rima-di, quiet as a prayer, fierce as a law; who loved across borders and kept that love a careful flame: you remain the guardian to all, and you show us steadiness is also bravery.

For dear Meghali – sharp-bright, the one who calls us to truth; who brews milk tea like memory and judgment like mercy, a leader who is always eventful: you remind us to be honest and kind in measured doses.

For our Dr. Ananya – whose kheer is comfort and whose laugh is home; calm like hues, who gives without ledger and forgives without ceremony: you teach us that generosity is dignity.

For our Niloy baba – who carries records, stories and abundance of information; the one who listens like a room and plays like a river: you hold our music when our mouths forget the words.

For beautiful Bidisha – new as dawn, steady as page, each smile unfolds page steady and kind: you remind us learning can be tenderness, and books can be arms or the mind.

For our boys Dhruv and Dimppan – jolly at heart, fit and full of jest, their impromptu jokes put tiredness to rest; like roadsters at dusk they steer us to safer tracks, keeping laughter on board and never looking back.

And for The Purples – a colour that keeps growing because we keep returning: may our threads knit deeper than distance; may our promises be louder than fear.

We are the colour that grown from calm and blaze, threads that return in many small ways.

Let's take these as coins for your pockets; take this as an oath—to be kind, to be honest, to be useful to each other and to the world."

Arunav let the last lines rest in the afternoon light. The room held its breath in little flutters: Rini's hand flew to her mouth, Zorika's tears leaked now openly, Meghali's jaw softened into a rare, wet smile. Garima's look was a quiet, tearful benediction. Niloy nodded, eyes bright. Ron's fingers dug into his palms and then released, as if to let an ache ease.

The spell broke with Dimppan's arrival—a clattering, triumphant return that scattered the hush. Bags and foil and steam announced the food's presence, and from the silence and emotions now the kitchen turned into celebration. Plates were laid as if following a sacred pattern: rice bowls, fish dishes, smoked pork tucked into corner plates, spicy chutneys like tiny firecrackers, and puris still puffing from the tawa. Laughter started again, this time thick and jubilant. Arunav's lines sat in the back of their throat like sweet residue—words that would be swallowed into memory.

They ate with the happy greed of friends who know meals like this are bridging gestures. Between mouthfuls came giggles and small confessions—Rini telling the story of her first date with Bidisha, adding a wry aside about a poet who liked Bidisha, Ron asking Garima again how she kept rotis soft—and the room made itself loud and human.

But the plateful joy did not smother the worry that had nudged them while they ate: **how to remain in regular touch?** SMSs and emails felt thin in a world turning digital at a speed they all felt. Arunav, who had always kept everyone threaded—goodnight messages, printed lists, careful itineraries—listened as someone proposed solutions. Could they make a communication group that was more than a line of messages? A place where photographs, short clips, plans, and small documents could live together? An online space that was private, safe, and constant?

Ideas started bubbling up—each suggestion met with quick nods and playful objections. The clock on the wall ticked toward one; Dhruv and Dimppan would leave at three with Arunav. The friends were still circling the question, a dozen good answers half-formed on the table between empty plates and steaming cups. They had shared a meal, a poem, and a little fear of distance; the rest—how to keep being The Purples across cities and flights—was a new kind of work, quiet and, they hoped, possible.

Outside the window a sliver of sunlight fell on the purple cushion where Rini had been sitting. The colour looked different now richer, because it was layered with everything they had said and eaten and felt today.

Chapter 20 –
The Orkut - a new digital world !

The house had the easy hum of a place that knew itself well: tea mugs half-full, a low pile of cushions, a cassette player waiting like an old friend. Zorika sat with a pen and a small notebook, scribbling a line she didn't want to forget. Ron, bent over a scrap of paper, was caught in his own creative quicks–ideas tumbling one after another in shorthand. Meghali crouched among a modest stack of cassettes, riffling through labels and little rewritable-charm recordings Arunav had made for them–curated playlists of afternoons and ruined romances and triumphant scenes. Meghali was busy finding the best cassette with some smoothie collections.

Rini was started writing the Slam book, one that Arunav brought last week, handed over to Ananya and requested to pass it on to everyone so that all feelings from each of them can be poured in words, both good and bad. It was already half filled from Ananya, Meghali, Zorika, Ron. Now it was Rini and Niloy's turn to complete the remaining pages.

So as Rini started into the slam book, she observed that Ananya had already poured her heart across several pages. The book, half-filled, smelled faintly of ink and friendship. Garima moved like water around the group, steady and patient.

Niloy—absorbed elsewhere, more a scholar than a poet—suddenly straightened. As he looked at the Slam book in Rini's lap, "Guys, guys, I found something. I heard of this new thing—Orkut. It's like a digital slam book, a place online where people keep profiles, friends, little notes, and communities." He smiled, proud in that way of someone who carries facts like tools.

Dhruv, lounging with his feet on a low stool, grinned. "Yeah, I've heard the name—never tried it though." "Digital slam book?" Zorika's voice rose, bright and incredulous. "How will that work?"

Garima's eyes lit. She moved to the desktop in the corner and, hands steady, fetched the old landline dongle from a drawer. The house had an internet provision—prepaid and precious—but they rarely used it; internet cafés were cheaper and more anonymous.

Today, though, it felt like the right moment to bring the web into their living room. Meghali plugged a cord with a careful hand; the modem coughed, blinked, and then, with the patient hiss of first connections, the desktop woke into the small square of the browser.

Garima, pragmatic and prompt, called John in Delhi for pointers. Being in Delhi, John had some better information about it, but he said let me gather more info and call you back shortly, he promised. They hovered over the screen with the hungry curiosity of people peeking into a new city through its main gate.

When John rang back–voice steady, a little amused–he explained Orkut in slices: a place to make a profile (photo, interests, a little "about me"), a friends list that grew like a digital roll-call, a "scrapbook" or "scraps" where people could leave public notes, and communities–spaces to gather people with similar tastes. There were testimonials, small paragraphs other people wrote about you; there were photo albums you could fill; and you could join communities, like clubs, to meet strangers who liked the same songs or food. Best of all for them: a community page where an entire friend-group could plant its banner and find each other again even when roads and cities pulled them apart.

"Let's make our accounts," Garima said, decisive.

"And a community – 'We are The Purples'..."

Soon the accounts were created one by one. They laughed at the profile names: Meghali chose something fierce and floral; Ron picked a handle that referenced the studio's first curtain; Zorika used a line from her best-known song; Rini, ever the romantic, wrote a short line from the poem she loved; Bidisha wrote with a quiet cleverness that made everyone nod; Niloy, wry and neat, signed as a student of the bureaucracy—half-joke, half-promise.

They took turns at the keyboard. Garima typed in the community's name while Arunav—watching, steady—helped frame the group description: "A ragged band of friends from Guwahati. We argue, we make food, we rescue each other's dignity. New members welcome. Purple is our colour....and this canvas is our home", with a purple shade on the page colour. It felt so right and apt: small, defiant, affectionate and representative of their friendships and the journey.

While the digital slam book grew pixel by pixel, the physical one did not go silent. Niloy—who had been teasing at prose between readings of ethics and public policy—picked up the pen. Where Rini had left a white margin, he wrote on the slam book. His words were tidy, a mix of wry observation and warm gratitude, a final neat entry that fit the book like a clean stamp: he thanked Arunav for friendship and for the little scaffolds of support that had kept him steady. Rini, hands slightly trembling now, added more lines of her own—lighter, tinged with mischief and longing. Bidisha, with a small, precise flourish, left a line that made everyone laugh in recognition, but then a few respectful lines that show their thankfulness to Arunav for what he did to her and Rini, that no one could do.

Chapter 21 –
It's time to logoff !

It was almost three. A clock ticked like a small, impartial judge.

Garima disappeared to the tiny kitchen and returned with a tray of cups—tea poured with that exacting love she reserved for evenings like this. The steam curled up between them, and it felt as if time softened around that smell.

Arunav, who had been quiet in the corner watching the small scene—the hands, the laughing mouths, the little domestic rituals—pulled from his bag a neat bundle wrapped in a bright cloth. He opened it gently, and inside each parcel was a friendship band—simple thread work, chosen colours braided with a care that read like a biography, purple is distinct in each band. He had made them himself as always, sourced careful with his heartfelt emotions: one for each friend.

"Advance Friendship Day," he said, voice catching a fraction, "I won't be here this year in this friendship day. Take this until I come back."

One by one they tied the threads to each other's wrists. There were whispered jokes about trends, murmured thanks, and hands that lingered for a beat longer than necessary. Then the moment gathered its gravity: they stood in a slow line and hugged him. Garima first—steady, maternal—then Ron, quick and warm, Bidisha, Rini, Meghali — tears and laughter braided into each embrace. Zorika hugged him as if she held his own teddy from past, never want to let him go for –a friend, a guide, a brotherly care she received throughout.

Niloy's hug was brief but firm, like a promise pinned to a sleeve. Dhruv and Dimppan, who had drifted in with last-minute checks and laughter, came to the door and clapped, theatrical and true.

Arunav took out his digital camera—his Digi cam, an old habit he kept like an heirloom—and set the timer. They clustered close, purple threads on wrists showing when arms tangled. The click caught them: a frozen second where cheeks were wet and smiles were honest, a portrait that held the whole weight of all their small, complicated lives. Meghali, ever prompt, uploaded the photo to their new Orkut page and, with a single keystroke, tagged them all.

Her message was fierce and delighted: *WE ARE THE PURPLES*. The page flickered with their names and the photo glowed like a new Sigel on the web.

They did not dwell long–none of them wanted to stretch the goodbye into a cliché–but the house felt thicker with what had been said and what had not. Arunav gathered his bag, zipped it with the same careful hands he had used to wrap the friendship bands. He moved toward the door; each step was a small tectonic shift.

At the threshold he turned, and for a moment there was no need for words. They lined up again, smaller, intimate, and blessed him in their own ways. The hugs happened anew–longer, a little less guarded. Ron adjusted something in his collar and offered a small, practical smile. Garima's fingers found his wrist and squeezed. Rini wiped her eyes with the back of her hand and laughed like someone who had just heard a very old, beautiful secret.

Outside, the lane waited with sunlight and the promise of bus noise and the long road.

Arunav stepped out, moved towards the jeep with Dhruv and Dimppan. The house behind him a soft shape of windows and laughter. The Purples stood at the doorway until the moving bus swallowed his figure and the lane returned to its everyday rhythm.

The house dissolved into a quieter kind of presence. Chairs kept their sleeping warmth; the cassette player suddenly felt necessary and precious; the pen that wrote on the slam book sat on the table as if asking for more ink. The Orkut community shimmered on a distant screen now—small profile pictures lined like flowers in a row—and the friendship bands lay loose on the table, their colours braided and bright.

They cleaned up slowly, a kind of domestic prayer. Meghali hummed under her breath; Zorika wrote a new line at the bottom of her notebook; Niloy reorganized a pile of papers as if filing the last hour into its proper place. Bidisha and Rini talked quietly about their public acceptance and place within the Purples; Ron and Garima made plans for the studio's next show.

As Niloy and Ron also needed to leave for their rooms, they stood once more in the middle of the room, looking at each other—their faces washed in the late afternoon light. The purple cushion by the window looked deeper now, layered with all that had been added over nights and days and small confessions. Bidisha—new and quietly fierce—looped her fingers through Rini's and smiled like someone who had just been let into a secret.

The house was both a place and a story: rooms that held laughter, a kitchen that had kept more than food, a book that contained confidences, and a new digital page that would hold the image of their leaving. The purple they claimed was not just a colour now; it was a weave of choices and memories–an inheritance they had made for themselves.

Arunav was gone. The door closed with that soft, inevitable sound of a chapter ending. The Purples gathered the last cups, folded the last napkins, and set the piles of cassettes on the shelf where it belonged: within reach, the digital page still glowing–*WE ARE THE PURPLES.*

Outside, the sky folded itself into a slow bruise of evening–indigo deepening toward the first stars–while inside the lamps woke like small moons, gilding the faces of the circle. They spoke in soft plans, threading future evenings together as one stitches a quilt: a book here, a steaming cup there, a camera's click, a song that comes round again–each a purple stitch in the long tapestry they were making. Friendship, in that room, felt less like a single harbour than a string of lanterns hung across the dark, each light a quiet promise to guide the other home.

A message appeared on the community page with a thumb up on the grouped photo: **"THE PURPLES – friendships stitched on a Purple Canvas"**; it was John Bungton from the other side, who unknowingly made this friendships' journey official with this name that would last forever.

"Keep a purple heart in your pocket – it will remind you where to find the way back."

Dear Readers:

Dear Reader – thank you for travelling to the last page with me. Your time and attention mean more than I can say. Though my writing journey is not new, but my journey as a published author is still at the beginning phase. So, the extent of my writing journey will be certainly dependent on the feedback, suggestions and criticism from my readers: your impressions, suggestions, and honest critiques will help shape future books. Please do share your feedback, ideas, or a review – my direct contact details are provided in the code below. I read every message and am grateful in advance for your thoughts.

With warm regards and thanks for your company on this road - Deep JB.

Deep JB